PUFFIN BOOKS

The Santa Clause

He couldn't wait to introduce his father. So as soon as Scott sat down, Charlie walked up to the front of the classroom.

'This is my dad, Scott Calvin,' he said.

'Hello, Mr Calvin,' droned the class.

'And what does your dad do?' asked the teacher, Ms Daniels.

'My dad is Santa Claus,' Charlie said proudly.

THE SANTA CLAUSE

A novel by DAPHNE SKINNER
Based on the motion picture from HOLLYWOOD PICTURES
Executive Producers RICHARD BAKER, RICK MESSINA and
JAMES MILLER
Based on the screenplay by LEO BENVENUTI & STEVE
RUDNICK
Produced by BRIAN REILLY, ROBERT NEWMYER and
JEFFREY SILVER
Directed by JOHN PASQUIN

PUFFIN BOOKS

PUFFIN BOOKS

Published by the Penguin Group
Penguin Books Ltd, 27 Wrights Lane, London w8 5tz, England
Penguin Books USA Inc., 375 Hudson Street, New York, New York 10014, USA
Penguin Books Australia Ltd, Ringwood, Victoria, Australia
Penguin Books Canada Ltd, 10 Alcorn Avenue, Toronto, Ontario, Canada m4v 3b2
Penguin Books (NZ) Ltd, 182–190 Wairau Road, Auckland 10, New Zealand

Penguin Books Ltd, Registered Offices: Harmondsworth, Middlesex, England

First published in the USA by Hyperion Books for Children 1994
Published in Puffin Books 1995
1 3 5 7 9 10 8 6 4 2

Puffin Film and TV Tie-in edition first published 1995

Text copyright © Hyperion Books for Children, 1994
Story, art and photographs copyright © Hollywood Pictures Company, 1994
All rights reserved

The moral right of the author has been asserted

Typeset by Datix International Limited, Bungay, Suffolk
Printed in England by Clays Ltd, St Ives plc
Filmset in 13/15 pt Monophoto Ehrhardt

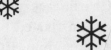

Chapter One

Charlie Calvin slumped in the back seat of his mother's car. As usual, they were parked outside his father's house, waiting, because, as usual, his dad was late. I just hope I can leave early, thought Charlie. It was hard enough spending weekends with Dad, but Christmas Eve? The worst. Charlie glanced at the single string of Christmas lights over Dad's front door. Typical. Every other house on the street was aglow with bright, blinking holiday decorations; angels, reindeer, even flamingos wearing Santa hats. But not Dad's house. One pathetic string of lights. And they were falling down.

Charlie sighed. His father definitely didn't have it together.

At last another car pulled up behind them. Scott Calvin got out and gave them a cheery wave. With a sigh, Charlie waved back half-heartedly and followed his mother out of the car.

'Laura! Charlie! Come in!' said Scott when they reached the porch. 'Hey, Sport, why don't you go look under the tree? There might be some things there for you.'

Charlie was glad to get away before his dad and his mum started bickering. He knew it was only a matter of time. But he could hardly believe what he found in the living room. A little fake tree with spindly blue branches. Under it, three lumpy packages wrapped in brown paper. Pathetic.

'So, what do you think, Sport?' his father asked when Charlie came back into the hallway.

Charlie tried not to sound too disappointed. 'There aren't that many presents there,' he mumbled.

'Well, Santa hasn't come yet,' said Scott.

'Neal doesn't believe in Santa,' said Charlie. Neal was his mum's new husband.

'Well, Neal's head comes to a point,' Scott snapped. He couldn't stand Neal.

'He's a doctor,' said Charlie. Personally, he thought Neal was cool.

Scott snorted. 'He isn't a doctor, Sport. He's a psychiatrist.'

Just then a horn honked outside. Neal.

Scott turned to his ex-wife angrily. 'Did that jerk tell Charlie there was no Santa?' he whispered.

'He only said that Santa Claus was more like a state of mind than a real person,' Charlie's mother answered.

'Kind of like Neal,' said Scott.

'We try to give Charlie a firm grasp on reality,' Laura replied, a little too loudly.

'Now that's a good idea,' answered Scott, raising his voice, too. 'We wouldn't want our kid running around using his imagination, now, would we?'

Charlie could feel his stomach knotting up. 'Why do you guys always have to fight?' he asked unhappily.

'We're not fighting, Sport,' said Scott. 'We're arguing. You see, Mom and Neal don't believe in Santa Claus because they've been naughty.' A wicked gleam came into his eyes. 'They're going to get a lump of coal in their stockings.'

'I don't know,' said Charlie. 'Seems kind of babyish to believe in that stuff.'

'Babyish!' exclaimed Scott. 'I believe in Santa, and I'm not a baby.'

The horn honked again. 'You'd better go,' Scott said to Laura. 'We wouldn't want to keep Doctor Brilliant waiting.'

Charlie and his mum hugged. 'I'll see you tomorrow,' she whispered.

'Do I have to stay?' Charlie whispered back. He wished he could leave with her. 'Will you pick me up tomorrow?'

'Of course I will.'

'Early?'

'You'll be fine,' she promised.

Charlie wasn't so sure.

A few hours later Charlie was even less sure. First his father burned the turkey so badly it looked like a flame-broiled meteorite. Then they had to drive around for ages searching for a place to eat. Charlie didn't know which was harder – finding an open restaurant on Christmas Eve or trying to talk to his dad.

His first big mistake was mentioning Neal. 'You know, Neal's a really good cook,' he said.

'Yeah, and he does his own dental work,' snapped Scott.

'You don't like him much, do you, Dad?' asked Charlie.

Scott's tone of voice softened a little. 'Oh, he's okay,' he said. 'There's just something about the guy that makes me want to . . .'

'. . . lash out irrationally?' said Charlie.

Scott looked at him. 'Where'd you hear that?'

'From Neal. I learn a lot from him,' said Charlie. 'He listens to me.'

'Yeah, but then he charges you for it,' said Scott, pulling up to a restaurant. It was closed. 'I listen,' he said. 'Don't I?'

Charlie just looked at him. Scott pulled away from the restaurant. 'You know, Charlie,' he said, 'you could learn stuff from me, too, if you came to visit more than just every other weekend.'

Charlie didn't say anything. What was there to say?

'We'd have a great time,' Scott said.

Charlie decided to set his father straight. 'We never have a great time,' he said flatly.

'How can you say that? Didn't I take you to the Bears game last weekend? That was fun!'

'No, it wasn't,' said Charlie. 'I don't even like football. I like soccer.'

'Soccer!' Scott said, as if it were a life-threatening disease. 'It's not even American! Only wimps play soccer.'

'I joined a team last month,' Charlie told him.

'You did?' said Scott. 'I didn't know that.'

That's because you don't want to know, thought Charlie.

Scott parked the car in front of a family-style restaurant. 'It's open!' he crowed. 'We're in luck!'

Charlie winced. 'I don't want to eat here,' he told his father.

'C'mon,' said Scott in an extra-jolly voice. 'Everybody likes this.'

'Disaster,' Charlie muttered as they walked inside. Naturally, his dad didn't even hear him.

After dinner they drove home in silence. Charlie changed into his pyjamas and climbed into bed, relieved that the evening was almost over. Then Scott announced he was going to read aloud.

'A story?' asked Charlie, surprised. His father never read to him.

'A poem,' said Scott. He started reading an old poem that began: ' 'Twas the night before Christmas . . .' It made Charlie drowsy, and his eyes closed. As they did, his father read, 'When out on the lawn there arose such a clatter, I sprang from my bed to see what was the matter . . .'

Charlie's eyes opened. 'What's that?' he asked.

'What's what?'

'*A rose suchak ladder*,' said Charlie. 'What is it?'

Scott smiled. 'Not a *ladder*,' he said. 'A *clatter*. A big noise. It means, "there came a big noise." ' He stroked Charlie's forehead. 'Time for you to go to sleep, Sport,' he said.

But Charlie had a few questions. 'How do reindeer fly?' he asked. 'They don't have any wings. And if Santa's so fat, how can he get down the chimneys? Besides, what about the people who don't have fireplaces? How does he get into their houses?'

'Look, Sport,' said Scott, 'believing in something means you just believe in it. Reindeer fly because that's how Santa gets around. You can't stop believing in things just because they don't make any sense.'

This was a new idea to Charlie. 'So, Dad,' he said, 'you really *do* believe in Santa?'

'Yeah, Sport,' said his father. 'I do.'

6

Charlie's eyes fell shut. 'Then we'd better leave some cookies and milk for him,' he said sleepily. 'Just in case . . .'

Scott grinned. 'Now you're talking,' he said. He felt better than he had all day.

Chapter Two

Later that night, the only sounds in the house were the hum of the refrigerator and the rumble of Scott's snoring. Charlie was fast asleep – until a loud thump from the roof woke him. He lay in bed listening. There it was again. Charlie got out of bed and found his way to Scott's room.

'Dad?' he said, shaking his father awake.

'What is it?' Scott asked, his voice somewhere between a croak and a yawn. His eyes stayed closed.

'I heard a clatter.' The thumping noise came again. 'There!' Charlie said. 'Don't you hear it? A clatter. A big noise. Coming from outside. Dad! I'm scared!'

'It's nothing,' snuffled Scott, turning over. 'Probably just the wind. Go back to sleep.'

Then the noise came again. This time it sounded as if half a dozen heavy barrels were dropping on to the roof. The house shook. Scott's eyes flew open, and he jumped out of bed.

He motioned to Charlie to be quiet. The ceiling

8

creaked. They looked at each other.

'Maybe it's Santa,' said Charlie.

'Not now, Charlie,' said Scott. He headed for the door. 'You wait here,' he said, 'and if you hear anything funny, dial nine-one-one, okay?'

Charlie nodded. He listened to his father walk downstairs and on to the back porch. For a moment there was total quiet. Then he heard his father shout, 'Hey, you!'

Charlie heard a slithering noise from the roof, followed by a soft thud. He ran downstairs and outside.

The moon hung in the sky like a big white ice-cream wafer, casting deep shadows around the house. Charlie saw his father standing next to a large, dark shape on the ground. Charlie drew closer. The shape was a man.

'Stay back, Charlie,' warned Scott. He pushed the man gently with his foot. There was no re-sponse – the man lay perfectly still. Grunting with effort, Scott slowly turned him over. Charlie saw with a shock that the man, who had a full white beard and a belly the size of a beach ball, was dressed in a Santa Claus suit. His red cap had slipped off his head, revealing silky white hair. He had bushy white eyebrows, and his round face wore a look of surprise.

'It *is* Santa, Dad!' cried Charlie. And then it hit him. 'You killed him!'

Scott winced. 'I did not,' he said. 'And he is not Santa Claus. This is a guy who was trying to break into our house. He fell off the roof.'

Charlie wasn't convinced. 'He looks like Santa.'

'He's got to have some ID on him,' said Scott, reaching into the man's pockets. The wallet he found had a business card in it. He and Charlie read it together: 'If something should happen to me, put on my suit. The reindeer will know what to do.'

Scott and Charlie looked at each other. Then they looked up at the roof. A large sleigh harnessed with eight reindeer stood next to their chimney. When they looked down again, the man had vanished. Only the Santa suit remained.

Charlie jumped up and down with excitement. 'You gonna put on the suit, Dad? Are you? Are you? Come on, Dad,' he demanded, 'put it on. 'Cause I wanna go, too!'

'Stop that, Charlie!' said Scott. 'We are not going anywhere!'

An all-too-familiar feeling of disappointment made Charlie's voice bitter. 'See?' he said. 'That's what I was talking about before. You never listen. Every time I want to do something, it's silly. You never do what I want to do. It's always what *you* want to do.'

Scott wondered if Charlie was right. He was so confused, he didn't know what to think. He started to pace back and forth. 'Okay,' he muttered to himself, 'reindeer on the roof. Santa suit on the lawn. The guy fell. Not my fault. Still, reindeer on the roof. Hard to explain. Very hard . . .' As he paced, he bumped into a ladder propped up against the side of the house – a ladder he had never seen before.

Charlie rushed over to examine it. 'Look here, Dad,' he said. 'Like the poem.'

A metal plaque on the ladder read, The Rose Suchak Ladder Company.

'Remember?' asked Charlie. 'It's from the poem you were reading to me tonight: "When out on the lawn there a rose suchak ladder"?'

'Yeah,' said Scott. 'From the poem.' He watched, confused, as Charlie began climbing up the ladder. Then he gathered up the Santa suit and followed slowly.

Moments later, they were on the roof. Eight very large, very restless reindeer looked at them with liquid black eyes. The largest, at the head of the team, pawed the roof impatiently.

'Easy, Rudolph,' said Scott.

The reindeer snorted and bucked. Its black eyes glittered.

Then Scott saw why. The tag around the animal's neck said 'Comet.'

'Whoops! Sorry, Comet,' said Scott. Comet stopped fidgeting, and his look said that he accepted the apology.

'Dad, check out Santa's sleigh!' said Charlie as he climbed in.

'This is *not* Santa's sleigh.' Scott tried to speak firmly.

'Well, what about the reindeer?'

'They . . . they're a gift from the cable company,' Scott said weakly. 'Merry Christmas. Now let's get off the roof.'

Scott laid the Santa suit on the seat of the sleigh and stepped in to lift Charlie out. But then, as if by secret signal, all the reindeer turned their faces to the sky. With a jingle of their bells, they bounded from the roof.

'Hold on, Charlie!' was all Scott had time to yell. And then he and Charlie found themselves flying through the glittering indigo sky in Santa Claus's sleigh.

Half an hour later they landed on the roof of a little house. Scott had got over feeling weird about what was happening. Not that he was having a good time – he just felt a little better about the situation. Easing in. And at least the reindeer seemed to know what to do. That was a relief.

So when they landed, Scott watched Comet for a cue. Sure enough, the big reindeer looked at him, and then at the bag sitting in the back of the sleigh.

'Toys!' said Charlie. 'He's telling you to get the bag of toys.'

'And do what?' said Scott.

'Go down the chimney,' said Charlie.

'You want me to get the bag of toys and go down the chimney into a strange person's house in my pyjamas?' spluttered his father.

'No,' Charlie explained patiently. 'You have to put the suit on first.'

'Of course,' said Scott sarcastically. 'I'll put the suit on first. Listen, Charlie, I'll tell you what we're going to do – we're going to get out of here. This whole thing is stupid!'

'Why is it everything I want to do is stupid?' Charlie burst out.

Scott was silent a moment before he spoke. 'I didn't say that,' he said. Then slowly he put on the huge red suit. When he was dressed, he clambered on to the roof and grabbed the bag. It was incredibly heavy. He slipped as he pulled it out of the sleigh, and Charlie cried out in alarm.

'I'm all right, Sport,' Scott said, though his voice was a little shaky. He leaned against the chimney to steady himself, wondering what to do next. How, for example, was he supposed to get down the chimney?

He didn't have much time to ponder the question. Instead, he simply started floating first up, then down. An image of an astronaut, tumbling end over end in deep space, flashed through his mind. Frightened, he waved his arms. And then, just as his son cried, 'Dad! You're flying!' he slithered down the chimney as if he were a new substance called Liquid Scott.

When he landed in the living room he felt solid again, solid enough to pull a doll, a toy rifle, and a pair of trainers out of his bag and set them under the tree. But the minute he laid them down, he heard a deep voice from upstairs.

'Who's down there?'

Panicked, Scott tried the nearest window, which immediately set off a loud security alarm. He rushed for the door. A large dog appeared in the doorway, growling. Now what do I do?! he thought.

He got his answer when he felt himself begin to reliquify. In seconds he was floating back up the chimney. Easy as can be.

Charlie, waiting in the sleigh, looked at him wide-eyed. 'Wow! Dad!' he said. 'How'd you do that? What'd it feel like?'

'Like . . . *America's Most Wanted*,' said Scott. 'Pull me in quick! We've got to get out of here.'

Scott flung his empty bag in the back of the sleigh and flopped down next to Charlie. He snapped the reins. 'Comet, let's go home!' he called. The reindeer vaulted into the sky.

But five minutes later they landed on another

roof. Scott was indignant. 'The bag's empty! There's nothing else!' he protested. Comet turned and growled at him. Could a reindeer growl? Comet definitely did.

'It's empty!' Scott insisted. He reached for the bag. 'Look –' He picked it up. It was full.

'Dad. Do it again,' said Charlie.

'But –' Scott started to protest. Then he was floating again. He panicked. 'Hold it!' he yelped. 'There's no chimney! Stop!'

Then he was Liquid Scott again, pouring down an exhaust vent into yet another house. When he landed he found himself standing in front of a mantelpiece and a fireplace. Where had they come from? Scott didn't know. And how had a doll and a basketball and a jack-in-the-box got into his bag? Scott didn't have a clue. He noticed a glass of milk and a couple of biscuits on the table, next to a plate of vegetables. Why fight it? he thought and stashed the biscuits and vegetables in his pockets.

It was only then that he noticed a little girl on the couch.

She sat up and rubbed her eyes. 'Santa?' she said. 'How come your clothes are so baggy?'

'Umm . . .' Scott hedged. 'Santa's watching his saturated fat.'

'Well, how come you don't have a beard?' the little girl persisted.

'I shaved!' said Scott. 'Now close your eyes and go to sleep.'

The little girl shut her eyes obediently. Scott sighed with relief and headed back to the chimney.

Once he was back in the sleigh again, he offered Charlie a biscuit. 'Hungry?' he asked.

'Starved!' Charlie said, and lunged for the biscuit. Scott ate one, too, and then another. For a few minutes the only sound in the silent night was the crunch of loud, happy chewing. Then Charlie and Scott became aware of another sound – the restless pawing of eight large reindeer.

'What's the matter, boy? You hungry, too?' Scott asked Comet. The reindeer tossed its head as if to say yes. Scott pulled some vegetables out of his pocket. 'Well, here you go,' he said, feeding Comet a carrot.

'Let me try!' Charlie scrambled out of the sleigh. Together, he and his father walked up the row of reindeer, feeding each one a carrot or a celery stick, murmuring its name, and giving it a pat on its warm neck. The reindeer, as big as horses, became quiet as Charlie fed them. Their dark eyes seemed much softer now, and a few actually nuzzled him as he passed. It sent an unexpected thrill through Charlie. He had never had much to do with animals before, and these were so big, and so friendly! *And* they could fly!

As if thinking the same thing, Scott announced,

'Well, there's work to be done, boys.' He climbed back into the sleigh, waited for Charlie to settle in next to him, and took up the reins. 'Now Dasher! Now Dancer! Now Prancer and Vixen!' he called. 'On Comet! On Cupid! On Donner and Blitzen!' Charlie's eyes widened. His dad sounded just like Santa Claus!

The reindeer thought so, too. They vaulted into the sky with a mighty leap, and Santa's sleigh was on its way once more.

Chapter Three

It had been a long night, thought Scott. Countless deliveries, down chimneys without number. Mountains of toys coming out of a seemingly bottomless sack. Endless Christmas trees. And pounds and pounds and pounds of biscuits.

Scott yawned. He was tired. So was Charlie, who was curled up next to him. It was dawn, and the sleigh had landed in a desolate white wasteland – cold, vast and empty.

'Is this okay, Dad?' asked Charlie nervously.

'Okay? No! It's not okay!' said Scott. He flapped the reins and called out, 'Hey, Comet! You made a wrong turn in Toronto! Now giddiup! Let's go home!'

Comet ignored him. For a moment the only sound Charlie and Scott heard was the keening of the wind. Then they heard something else. Footsteps. They looked around.

A tiny figure was trudging towards them through the snow. As Scott and Charlie watched, the figure came closer. It was an elf, three feet high, dressed in red and green. Without saying a word, he walked up to Comet, took hold of the harness, and urged the reindeer forward. The sleigh started to move.

'Is *this* okay, Dad?' asked Charlie.

'I think so, Sport,' said Scott. 'I mean, he's only an elf, right?' He called out to the tiny man. 'Hello?' There was no answer. He tried again. '*Habla inglés?*' By this time the elf had led them to a snowdrift. He reached into it and pulled up a red-and-white-striped pole.

'What's that?' wondered Scott.

'I think we're at the North Pole,' said Charlie. The elf found the numeric keypad on the pole and punched in a four-digit code. Nothing happened. He tried again. Nothing. Looking annoyed, the elf pulled a piece of paper out of his pocket, read the code on it, and tried again.

Suddenly Scott and Charlie heard a high, whining noise, almost like a lift. Then they were spiralling down – sleigh, reindeer, elf, and all – in a dizzying rush of wind, mist, and snow.

When they landed and opened their eyes, they were in a huge enclosed area, rather like an aeroplane hangar. A crowd of elves immediately rushed over to the sleigh. They were small, serious-looking men and women wearing red and green clothing and intent expressions. Their skin, Scott noticed with surprise, had gold flecks in it. Surprisingly, too, many of them looked young. Some started to clean and polish the sleigh. Others began to groom the reindeer. No one said a word to Scott or Charlie.

Puzzled, Scott walked up to one of them. 'Excuse me,' he said. 'Who's in charge here?'

The elf bowed at him. 'You are.'

'No,' said Scott, 'I mean, of you guys. Who's in charge?'

'You are,' the elf repeated.

'That's not what I mean!' said Scott. 'Who's the head elf?!'

'You are,' the elf said calmly, for the third time.

Scott just stood there. Was there some mysterious elf language – Elfish? – that he just didn't understand? He was just about to try again when another elf, a slightly taller one, approached. He looked young, but had a stern face and the air of someone who's used to giving orders.

'Who's causing all the trouble around here?' he asked.

'He is,' said the first elf, pointing at Scott.

'Who are you?' asked Scott.

'I'm Bernard,' said the elf. 'Nice to meet you, Santa.'

'I'm not Santa!' Scott half-yelled.

'The other Santa is . . . gone, right?'

'Yes, but . . .,' Scott began, but the elf turned abruptly and motioned for him to follow.

Bernard headed through the hangar and down a

long hallway with many doors leading off on either side.

'It wasn't my fault,' Scott tried to explain as he hurried along behind the elf. 'That other guy fell. It was an accident . . .'

Bernard didn't seem to be listening. 'Can I get you a drink?' he asked politely.

Before Scott could answer, Charlie interrupted. '*I'm* thirsty. And hungry,' he said.

The elf spun around. 'Who's this?' he asked.

'My son, Charlie,' said Scott.

Bernard's stern face broke into a smile. 'Hiya, Sport,' he said.

Charlie liked him right away. 'Hey, Dad, he called me Sport,' he said. 'Just like you!'

'Why not?' said Bernard. 'You look like a Sport. Here, I've got something for you,' he said, handing Charlie a glass snowball.

There was a row of tiny plastic houses inside the ball, each with its own Christmas tree.

'Shake it up, Charlie,' said the elf.

Charlie turned the ball over. Slowly it began to pulse with light, as if it were coming alive. And then it did come alive! Snow began to fall, people appeared at the windows of all the tiny houses, and Santa flew across the sky! The people waved up at his sleigh, and all the lights on the street twinkled. More snow fell, like a curtain of lace. Then it stopped, and the tiny scene went dark.

Charlie had never seen anything so beautiful. 'Wow!' he whispered, handing it back to Bernard.

'Why don't you hold on to it for a while,' said the elf. When Charlie hesitated, Bernard added, 'Go on. I trust you to keep it safe.'

'What do you say, Charlie?' said Scott, who hadn't seen the ball come alive.

'Thanks! I promise I'll take really good care of it,' said Charlie.

'I know you will,' said Bernard. He beckoned to one of the elves. 'Larry, take Charlie with you and get him some food.' Then he walked back over to Scott. 'Follow me,' he said. 'You'll be wanting to get out of those clothes.'

Scott followed Bernard through a door marked Workshop, where more elves sat at long, low benches, busily making toys. 'I'll be wanting to go home!' he said, annoyed. Who did this little guy with the big attitude think he was, anyway? And why did he keep insisting Scott was Santa Claus?

'Now, look,' Scott tried again. 'I'm not Santa!'

'Did you or did you not read the card?' asked Bernard, stern once more.

'Well, yes I did, but –'

'Then you are the new Santa Claus,' Bernard told him. 'By putting on the hat and jacket you accepted the contract.'

Scott was confused. 'What contract?' he asked.

'The Santa Clause,' said Bernard, 'on the card

you pulled out of Santa's wallet. Do you still have it?'

Scott found the card in his pocket and handed it to the elf.

'See? Right here in fine print,' said Bernard. He started reading it to Scott. '"The Santa Clause: In putting on this suit and entering the sleigh, the wearer waives any and all rights to any previous identity, real or implied, and fully accepts the duties and responsibilities of Santa Claus in perpetuity until such time that the wearer becomes unable to do so either by accident or design." The Santa Clause,' he concluded. 'It's all very standard.'

'That's ridiculous!' Scott protested. 'I'm not –'

But Bernard didn't want to hear it. 'Try to understand this,' he snapped. 'Toys have to be delivered. I'm not going to do it, because it's not my job. It's Santa's job. But Santa fell off a roof – your roof!' He stepped closer to Scott and scowled up at him. 'You read the card,' he snarled. 'You put on the suit. That clearly falls under the Santa Clause. So now *you* are Santa. Okay?'

Something told Scott it was useless to argue. Bernard was looking less like an elf and more like a pit bull every minute. 'You leave for home tomorrow morning,' he snapped. 'You've got eleven months – until Thanksgiving – to get your affairs in order. Then you're due back here. I'll ship the list to your house.'

23

'What list?' asked Scott.

The elf gave him an I-don't-believe-you look. 'Come on,' he said. 'The *list*. As in, "He's making a list . . ."'

'". . . and checking it twice,"' said Charlie, who came running up to his father with his mouth full of biscuits.

'That's right, Sport,' said Bernard. He turned back to Scott. 'You put a *P* next to the kids who were nice and a *C* next to the ones who were naughty.'

'*P* and *C*?' asked Scott.

'*P* for present. *C* for coal, right?' asked Charlie.

Bernard winked at him.

Scott was puzzled. 'How am I supposed to know who's —'

'You'll know,' Bernard assured him.

'And what if I decide I don't want to do this?'

Bernard looked shocked. 'Don't even joke about a thing like that,' he said.

'Why not?' demanded Scott. 'What if I don't buy into this . . . "clause"? What if I choose not to believe it?'

All sound in the Workshop stopped. Bernard stepped closer to Scott, his eyes glittering with anger. 'Then there would be millions of disappointed children around the world,' he said quietly. 'Children hold the spirit of Christmas in their hearts. You wouldn't want to be responsible for killing the spirit of Christmas, *now would you*?' He jabbed Scott's stomach with a tiny finger. Scott, taken aback, was speechless.

Which was fine with Bernard, who started to march off, then stopped and added, 'Judy will take you to your room. Get out of the suit. It needs to be cleaned. Then get some sleep. We've got a lot of work to do in a year.'

Judy was much nicer than Bernard, thought Scott. She had a friendly face. She didn't yell at him. She called him 'sir,' and she even brought him a cup of delicious hot cocoa as he was getting ready for bed.

And when he sat there in Santa's bedroom, dressed in Santa's very own red silk pyjamas, Judy listened thoughtfully to Scott's confession.

'I stopped believing in Santa Claus a while ago,' he told her, his voice troubled.

She patted his back. 'Not surprising,' she said. 'Most grown-ups have a hard time believing in magic.'

'Listen, let's be honest,' Scott said. 'This is a dream. You're a dream. I mean, I'm seeing this and I can't believe it.'

'You're missing the point,' said Judy. 'Seeing isn't believing. *Believing is seeing.* Kids don't have to see this place to know that it's here. They just know.'

Somehow Judy's words made Scott feel better. He also felt, suddenly, very, very tired. Judy wished him goodnight, and he settled back into bed with an enormous yawn. An instant later, he was sound asleep.

Chapter Four

'Dad! Dad!' Scott woke abruptly to the sound of Charlie's voice calling from the hallway. 'You should see all the toys,' cried his son, bursting into the bedroom. 'Come on, get up. Get up!'

There was no time to think about his unusual red silk pyjamas or his strange dream of elves and sleighs and reindeer because Charlie was pulling him downstairs into the living room, where a mountain of brightly wrapped presents lay under the tree. Scott had no idea where they'd come from; Charlie didn't care. He just started to open them as fast as he could.

Then the doorbell rang, and Charlie ran to answer it. 'Mom!' he cried, greeting Laura happily.

'Did you have a good time?' she asked, surprised at his cheerful expression. Usually he couldn't even manage a smile when she picked him up at Scott's. Today he was beaming.

'A great time!' he told her. 'Dad and me and the reindeer flew up to the North Pole. Dad was

Santa, and Larry showed me the Workshop. It was neat, Mom, really! You should have been there.'

Laura glared at Scott, who stood there bleary-eyed in his red pyjamas. She sent Charlie out to the car, where Neal was waiting, and then turned to her ex-husband.

'Scott!' she hissed. 'What kind of stories have you been filling Charlie's head with? The North Pole! Santa! Really!'

Scott scratched his head. 'I'm not filling his head with anything,' he said. 'I thought it was a dream . . .'

Then it hit him. How could it have been a dream if Charlie knew about the Workshop and the elves? He ran out to the car.

'Sport!' he said to Charlie, who was in the back seat. 'Who showed you the Workshop?'

'Larry,' said Charlie matter-of-factly.

'What was the other one's name?' asked Scott.

'Bernard.'

'And who gave me the pyjamas?'

'Judy,' said his son. 'Why?'

'What's this all about?' asked Neal with a frown.

'Dad took me to the North Pole,' Charlie told him. 'He's the new Santa, because the regular Santa fell off our roof.'

Scott stood there, dumbfounded. 'But it was a dream,' he said.

Laura and Neal scowled at him and then drove away. 'It couldn't have happened,' he yelled after them. But as he watched them disappear down the street, he wrestled with a thought so incredible that it made his scalp tingle. Maybe his dream wasn't really a dream. Maybe the Santa Clause was real!

A few weeks later, Scott sat in the conference room of the B and R Toy Company staring at the plate of biscuits across the table. Ever since Christmas, Scott had found himself on a new diet – the Milk and Biscuits Diet – and his craving for biscuits seemed to be getting stronger with every passing day.

The sight of an entire plate of chocolate chip biscuits just out of his reach was very frustrating. He'd been signalling for them over and over again! But no one at the table noticed. All eyes were on the boss, Mr Whittle, as he made a speech about a new B and R toy.

'It is with much pleasure and pride that I announce our next best-seller,' he boomed. 'B and R's Total Tank. This is our high-end male action toy for next Christmas, which we hope to retail at $159.00 . . .'

As Mr Whittle droned on, Scott forgot about the biscuits, the meeting, and the high-end action toys. He began to doodle a glass snowball, just like the one Bernard had given Charlie at the North Pole. As he drew, he could almost swear he heard bells jingling – sleigh bells . . .

Then all of a sudden he heard his name being called. He looked up.

The entire room was staring at him. Mr Whittle was staring especially hard. Scott didn't like that look. It meant something was wrong.

'Yes, Mr Whittle?' he asked innocently, dropping his pencil.

'The Total Tank focus group, Scott?' said Mr Whittle.

'Yes, sir,' said Scott. 'It was last week.'

'I *know*! Do you have the report?' Mr Whittle's face was turning all blotchy and red.

'Yes, I do.' Scott shuffled through his papers. 'I, uh . . . I must have left it in my office,' he said.

'Well, if it wouldn't be too much trouble,' said Mr Whittle, 'would you find it and bring it to us, since *we are all waiting*?'

Scott jumped to his feet. 'Sorry. Be right back with it.' As he left the room, he turned back for a moment. 'Anyone else hear those bells?' he asked.

Dead silence.

'The report,' said Scott. 'Right. I'll be back in a second.'

Ever since their night in the sleigh, Charlie felt

different about his dad. He used to pity him for messing up so much. He was angry with him a lot, too, for the same reason. But after seeing him deliver all those presents, Charlie began to feel proud of his dad. After all, he had an incredibly important job to do! Maybe the most important job of anyone!

So when Scott walked into his classroom on Career Day, Charlie was really surprised and pleased. There were other parents there, too, of course, including Charlie's mum and Neal. But their jobs weren't half as interesting as Scott's. Not that there was anything wrong with being a psychiatrist like Neal. Charlie even used to think it was kind of cool. And his mum's job, travel agent, was fine too. But now they seemed a little ordinary to Charlie.

Nothing like being Santa.

He couldn't wait to introduce his father. So as soon as Scott sat down, Charlie walked up to the front of the classroom.

'This is my dad, Scott Calvin,' he said.

'Hello, Mr Calvin,' droned the class.

'And what does your dad do?' asked the teacher, Ms Daniels.

'My dad is Santa Claus,' Charlie said proudly.

Everyone started laughing. Scott jumped up. He had seen the looks of outrage on Neal's and Laura's faces. He had to do something fast.

31

'I think what Charlie means,' he said to everyone, 'is that I'm *like* Santa.'

'That's *not* what I mean, Dad,' said Charlie. He turned to the class. 'Look, on Christmas Eve my dad pushed Santa off the roof. Santa disappeared and my dad took his place. Then the reindeer flew us to the North Pole, where the head elf, Bernard, gave me this.' He pulled the glass ball from his backpack.

Scott interrupted. 'Listen,' he said to the class, 'I work for a toy company. And in a way I deliver toys all over the country, like Santa . . .'

'Do you make the toys?' asked a girl from the back of the room.

'No, stupid,' sneered Bobby Turrell, a kid who had two jobs: class know-it-all and class bully. 'The *elves* do.'

The class laughed again. 'The toys are made somewhere else,' Scott explained. 'At a factory overseas.'

Bobby ignored his answer. 'So, let me get this straight,' he jeered. 'If I want to be Santa when I grow up, all I have to do is push you off a roof?'

The class burst into laughter again.

But Scott noticed Laura and Neal weren't laughing.

The next morning Scott sat in the principal's office with Laura and Neal. He tried to explain.

'First of all,' he said, 'I didn't push Santa. He fell.'

Laura was outraged. 'Why are you doing this, Scott?' she asked. 'Why's Charlie making up all these stories? Why's he saying this is the best Christmas he's ever had?'

'He said that?' Scott was surprised – and touched.

'After everything you've told him? Of course he did!'

'This is far more serious than a boy believing or not believing in Santa Claus,' Principal Compton interrupted.

'Charlie thinks it really happened,' Laura added.

'Look,' said Scott in his most reasonable tone of voice. 'It *was* Christmas, right? So it makes sense that I had some holiday fantasy pop into my head. I must have told Charlie. He must have liked it. End of story.'

'And did you go to the North Pole?' asked Neal accusingly.

'This is ridiculous,' said Scott.

'Ridiculous or not,' said the principal, 'for Charlie this isn't some dream. It's real. You need to sit down with Charlie, Mr Calvin. Explain to him that you're not Santa Claus and *get through to him*. No matter what it takes.'

Scott got the message. He was going to have a little talk with Charlie. Soon.

Chapter Five

The following Saturday, Scott and Charlie were together again, and Scott meant to talk to his son. But not right away – he didn't want to spoil their day. Scott had brought home a new Total Tank toy so that he and Charlie could assemble it together. And now, here they were, in the living room, trying to do just that. But they weren't getting very far.

The Total Tank had about nine million little parts, and they were scattered all over the floor. The instruction book was as thick as a phone book and a lot more confusing.

'I hate kits,' announced Charlie. 'They have millions of parts that never work. They break ten seconds after you build them. And you always end up spending more money to get new parts.'

'But the important thing is that we're doing this together,' said Scott, trying to sound enthusiastic. Charlie's response was a yawn and a grunt.

After an hour of trying to follow the instructions, even Scott had to admit defeat. There were nine wing nuts instead of ten. He couldn't tell the difference between the driveshaft and the wheelbase. And Charlie, totally bored, was watching television.

'Hey, Sport, I feel like going out,' Scott said finally. 'What do you say we go to the zoo?'

Fifteen minutes later they were walking past the reindeer pen, heading for the polar bears.

'These are just like the bears at the North Pole,' said Charlie, staring wistfully at the big shaggy creatures.

Here's my chance! thought Scott. 'Charlie,' he began, 'I've already told you we never went to the North Pole. Remember? It was all just a dream.'

'Nah,' said Charlie. 'It happened.'

Scott kept trying. 'I can't explain it,' he said. 'But I know what happened wasn't real.'

'It *was* real,' said Charlie.

'How do you know?' demanded Scott. 'There's no proof. So why don't we just say it was a great dream and forget it?'

'Proof?' Charlie smiled. 'What about this?' He held out the glass ball Bernard had given him, the one that lit up and had snow falling inside it. It wasn't lit up now, though.

Scott turned the ball over in his hands. 'This is just a cheap toy,' he said. 'We used to make these at B and R. Years ago.'

Charlie knew the ball was magic. If his dad

couldn't see it now, he would before too long. Just the way he'd realize he was Santa. He had to.

'I know who you are, Dad,' he said. 'You'll figure it out soon enough. There are a lot of kids who believe in you. You can't let them down.'

Scott's heart sank. He wasn't getting anywhere. 'Charlie, you're wrong,' he protested. To his surprise, his son was smiling again.

'What's so funny?' he asked.

'Nothing,' said Charlie. There was no way he'd tell his father that eight reindeer, zoo reindeer, were lined up in pairs behind them. Had they jumped over the fence of their pen? Or flown over? Who knew? But one thing was dead certain to Charlie. The reindeer were following his dad. Correction, he thought. The reindeer are following Santa. His grin got even wider.

So much for our little talk, thought Scott.

A few weeks later Scott found himself having another little talk. This one wasn't with Charlie. It was with Mr Whittle, his boss. In its way, it was just as disturbing.

It started off with Mr Whittle complaining. He'd been doing a lot of that lately. This time he was upset because Scott was eating milk and biscuits instead of sending out the Christmas orders of Total Tanks.

'I just got off the phone with Dale Jenkins,' Mr

Whittle said, 'and he told me something I couldn't believe. He told me you haven't shipped him the Total Tank yet.'

Scott sat at his desk and munched on a biscuit. 'Oh, yes,' he said. 'I was going to talk to you about that.'

'Talk?' exclaimed Mr Whittle. 'What is there to talk about? He's a toy buyer. We send him a toy and he buys!'

Scott picked up the glass ball that sat on his desk. 'Well, you know, Mr Whittle,' he said, 'I was looking at the Tank and I was wondering . . . is it really the kind of toy an eight-year-old would like?'

Mr Whittle opened his mouth to answer. Then he noticed the ball in Scott's hands. 'What's that?' he asked.

'It's my son's,' said Scott. 'We used to make them here. Why did we stop?'

Mr Whittle stared at Scott. His pale blue eyes widened, and his round, puffy face turned red. He looked like a fifty-year-old baby getting ready to scream.

'Why?' he answered loudly. 'I'll tell you why! Because it doesn't shoot, explode, kill, or talk. It doesn't change into anything, fly, drive, glow in the dark, ooze, or stick to the walls, that's why! It just sits there! *Now send that sample*!'

And he stormed out.

*

37

A few days later, Neal decided it was his turn to try to have a talk with Charlie. He sat next to his stepson on the living room couch, being as reasonable as he could. But Charlie just didn't seem to want to listen to what he was saying. No matter how logical it was.

Neal picked up a globe. 'Let's try again.' Pointing to the top, he said, 'Here's the North Pole. And here's the rest of the world.' He pointed again. 'Now, how can one man visit all the children of the world in one night? It isn't logical. It's impossible.'

'Not everyone celebrates Christmas,' said Charlie.

'And that upsets you?' asked Neal. Maybe Charlie was listening to him after all.

'No,' said Charlie. 'Not everyone celebrates Christmas. So Santa doesn't have to visit *everyone*.'

Neal sighed. 'Well, what about fireplaces?' he asked. 'A lot of people don't have them. How does Santa visit those people?'

'He turns into Jell-O and a fireplace just kind of appears,' said Charlie without hesitation.

'Okay,' said Neal. 'What about the reindeer? Have you ever seen reindeer fly?' he asked a little desperately.

'Yes.'

'Well, I haven't,' said Neal.

'Have you ever seen a million dollars?' asked Charlie.

'No.'

'Just because you haven't seen it doesn't mean it doesn't exist,' said Charlie with irrefutable logic.

This is really out of control, thought Neal. At that moment Scott and Laura appeared in the doorway. Scott had stopped by to pick up Charlie for the afternoon.

'Hi, Sport,' he said to his son. 'Feel like taking a walk with your old man?'

Charlie was glad to see him. 'Do I ever,' he said. 'I'll get my jacket.'

Charlie dashed out of the room. Scott turned to follow, but Laura stopped him.

'Scott, how can you tell these ridiculous stories to Charlie?' she asked. 'You *have* to tell him the truth.'

'The truth . . .?' But I don't know what the truth is, thought Scott. Maybe I *am* Santa Claus!

'Yes, be honest with him, Scott,' said Neal. He and Laura exchanged worried glances. 'Because I'm really concerned.'

'About what?' asked Scott, bristling.

'About whether it's good for Charlie to spend time with you,' said Neal.

It was a threat, and Scott knew it.

Chapter Six

Later that afternoon Scott and Charlie sat across the street from the house they had lived in before Scott and Laura's divorce.

'Funny,' said Charlie. 'It looks smaller to me now.'

'Maybe you're just bigger,' said Scott.

'Yeah,' agreed Charlie. 'Hey!' he added. 'By next year, I'll be big enough to fly the sleigh all by myself!'

Scott winced. 'No!' he protested.

'Okay, okay,' said Charlie. 'The year after.'

'No. That's not what I meant.' Scott took Charlie by the shoulders. 'Sport,' he said, 'we've got to get something straight about this Santa business. There is no –' He couldn't finish.

'No what?'

The words *There is no Santa Claus* refused to come out of Scott's mouth. Instead, he said, 'There is no reason why you should tell people about the North Pole.'

'Why not?'

Scott didn't want to tell Charlie to lie. 'Well, because sometimes there are things . . . big things . . . that are better left unsaid.'

'You mean like a secret?' asked Charlie.

'YES!' exclaimed Scott. 'That's it! A secret. Right!' He looked his son in the eye. 'Let's keep it a secret.'

'Why?' asked Charlie.

'Well, you know, Mom and Neal feel . . . And not just Mom and Neal . . . There's the school – not that it's important what they think, but you know . . .' Scott's voice trailed off for a moment. 'I need you to do this for me, Sport,' he said finally. 'Will you? Please?'

Charlie was flattered. His father had never asked him for anything before. This would be hard, but he'd do it. 'Sure, Dad,' he said.

Scott beamed with relief. Finally, he thought, life would be normal again.

But Scott was wrong.

Things were far from normal, as he found out the next morning.

His weight, for instance, had suddenly jumped to 190 pounds. His normal weight was 160. His hair was turning grey, and he had grown a beard – overnight! Scott didn't understand it, and he didn't like it.

He had other problems, too. Big ones. None of his clothes would fit, and he was late for an important

41

meeting. He had to race to the office dressed in an old tracksuit that was much too small for him. And once he was actually at the meeting, things got even worse.

Everyone there looked shocked when he came into the conference room, so he told them he was dressed casually because his dry-cleaners had burned to the ground – with all his clothes in it.

Then Mr Whittle asked him how he'd put on so much weight, and he had to make up another story, this time about having an allergic reaction to a bee sting.

He could tell no one believed him, either. It was terrible.

It was terrible, too, when they all ordered lunch. Because even though he meant to order sensible, healthy food like everyone else – Caesar salad, no dressing – when the waiter came to him, Scott heard himself asking for biscuits, a hot fudge sundae with extra fudge, and an order of cheese-cake on the side. Everyone stared at him, horrified.

It got worse.

The purpose of the meeting was to look at the plans for the new Total Tank TV commercial. Like all toy advertisements, this one cost a lot of money, and everyone took it very seriously – the people from B and R, and the man from the advertising agency.

It began with a shot of Santa Claus at the North Pole, and as soon as Scott saw it he laughed.

Silence fell over the conference room.

'Is there a problem?' asked the man from the ad agency.

'No, nothing,' said Scott. 'Nothing.' Unfortunately, he couldn't stop there. 'It's a little thing,' he added. 'The elves.'

'What about them?'

'They look funny,' said Scott.

'They're supposed to. They're elves,' said the advertising man curtly.

'I know that,' said Scott. 'But they should look younger. And their skin should have gold flecks in it.'

'Pardon me?' said the advertising man.

'You know, gold flecks in their skin,' Scott said again, as if this were common knowledge about elves.

The advertising man chose not to answer Scott. Instead he turned to the second shot in the commercial, a picture of Santa in the Total Tank. 'This year,' he said proudly, 'Santa's not going in his sleigh. He's going in a Total Tank! We think it's a great concept.'

'Now wait a minute,' said Scott. All heads swivelled his way. 'Not that *I* know anything about Santa Claus,' he continued, 'but there is *absolutely no way* Santa would give up his sleigh.'

'He would if he was trying to sell the Total Tank,' said the advertising man, shooting Mr Whittle an I-don't-believe-this-joker look.

Scott ignored him. 'Look, he needs his reindeer, right? Who do you think knows the way to all those houses but the reindeer? Santa can't do all those things himself. I mean, after all, he's only human – I guess.'

'Calvin!' interrupted Mr Whittle.

'I'm not finished!' Scott was standing now, addressing everyone in the room. 'While we're discussing the Total Tank,' he said, 'have any of you tried putting it together?' He looked around the room. No one said a word. 'Well, let me tell you: nuclear fusion is simpler. Even if you do manage to assemble the thing, it doesn't work. It breaks ten seconds after you build it. So you have to spend even more money on new parts. Ridiculous.'

'Calvin!' Mr Whittle got to his feet a little unsteadily and glared at Scott. 'I'd like to see you outside –'

'What we should try to come up with,' Scott went on, 'is a simple, basic, affordable toy. Something that nurtures creativity –'

'NOW!' exploded Mr Whittle. Grabbing Scott by the collar of his tracksuit, he dragged him into the hallway. 'I don't know what's gotten into you, Calvin,' he fumed. 'You're fat. That beard is a

"Hey, you!" Scott shouts at the man who's fallen from the roof and is lying in the snow.

Scott and Charlie can't believe their eyes! A large sleigh harnessed with eight reindeer is standing next to their chimney.

Eight reindeer and a sleigh on the roof? This is going to be the best Christmas Eve ever!

It is Christmas Eve, and little does Scott know that once he dons the huge red Santa suit, there's no turning back!

"Whoa!" Without even trying, Scott floats up into the sky and slithers down the chimney to deliver his first bagful of toys.

On solid ground again, Scott is glad not to feel like *Liquid Scott* anymore!

"Now, Dasher! Now, Dancer! Now, Prancer and Vixen! On, Comet! On, Cupid! On, Donner and Blitzen!"

Bernard gives Charlie a magic glass snowball.

Bernard explains the Santa Clause to Scott.

Scott thinks this whole night is just a dream, but is he willing to take the chance of disappointing millions of children around the world?

Becoming rounder and rounder and more Santa-like every day, Scott wonders why the B and R Toy Company doesn't make good toys like the glass ball anymore.

Charlie can do anything he sets his mind to.... Believing is seeing!

In Santa's bedroom at the North Pole, rows and rows of portraits of previous Santas, trapped by the Santa Clause, adorn the walls.

Laura's, Charlie's, and Neal's Christmas dreams all come true!

Charlie can be with his dad—the one-and-only Santa Claus—anytime he misses him. All he has to do is shake the magic glass snowball!

disgrace. And you're acting crazy. I mean, *gold flecks*?!'

'You're right,' said Scott apologetically. 'I don't know what got into me.'

'Well, do something about it,' said Mr Whittle. 'Go see a doctor or something. Get some help. Soon!'

Dr Meyers had been treating Scott and the Calvin family for years. He was a plump, easygoing man who gave all his patients chocolate lollipops. Scott liked him.

And he liked hearing what Dr Meyers had to say. 'Scott, you're healthy as a horse. What's the problem?'

Scott smiled, relieved. 'No problem, really,' he said. 'Actually, I'm feeling great.' He waited for his chocolate lollipop.

But Dr Meyers wasn't quite finished with him. 'You've put on some weight since I saw you last year,' he said. 'What's your diet like?'

'Mostly biscuits and milk,' confessed Scott. He liked to think of it as a vegetarian diet, only better.

'Well, there it is,' said the doctor. 'Try to cut back on the sweets, okay?' He smiled at Scott. 'Anything else?'

'There is one thing,' said Scott. 'How fast should facial hair grow?' He rubbed his full beard.

45

'It varies from person to person,' said the doctor. 'Why?'

'Well . . . I shaved this morning.'

Dr Meyers frowned and checked Scott's thyroid gland. 'Hmmm . . . normal,' he murmured. 'Try another kind of razor, I guess.'

'Also,' said Scott, 'as you can see, my hair's turned grey.'

The doctor smiled. 'You can dye it,' he said. 'Now let's take a listen to the old ticker, okay?'

Dr Meyers put the stethoscope to Scott's chest. Scott's heart sounded normal – at first. But after a moment the rhythm changed. Dr Meyers' eyes widened as he listened. There was no mistaking it. Scott's heart was pumping out the tune to 'Jingle Bells'.

Chapter Seven

Several weeks later, on a Saturday in early spring, Scott decided to stroll over to the park. Now that he'd seen Dr Meyers, he'd stopped worrying. It was a beautiful day, and he was on his way to watch Charlie play football.

When Charlie saw Scott, he ran right over to him. 'Hey, Dad, what're you doing here?' he asked, sounding surprised. He looked pleased, too. His father had never bothered to come to the football field before.

'I dunno,' said Scott. 'I thought I'd see what this soccer stuff is all about. Lots of people play it, right? Including you. So it must have something. And I kind of like the idea of seeing you bounce a ball off your head, Sport.' He grinned.

Charlie grinned back. 'This is great, Dad,' he said. 'You can come whenever you want.'

Just then a pink rubber ball bounced by Scott's feet. A dark-haired girl came running after it. Scott picked up the ball, tossed it to the girl, and called, 'There you go, Ruth.'

'Thanks,' she said, a little startled.

Charlie stared at his father. 'How did you know her name?' he asked.

'Gee, I don't know,' said Scott. He scratched his head, just as puzzled as Charlie. 'Look,' he said, 'I'll just go sit over there on that bench. Where that other little girl is sitting.'

'Fine.' Charlie ran back to his game, and Scott settled down to watch. But before two minutes had passed, he realized that the little girl on the bench was staring at him. Hard. She had curly red hair and a band of freckles across her nose.

'What is it?' he asked her.

She climbed on to his lap. 'I want some ballet shoes,' she whispered into his ear.

And she was just the first. Before Scott knew how or why, there was a line of kids waiting beside his bench. One by one they climbed on to his lap and told him what they wanted for Christmas. A few were shy, a few were funny, and one or two seemed to want half the toys made in the United States. But the surprising thing was that Scott knew everyone's name, and he liked them all. Not a single lump of coal in the bunch, he thought, smiling.

Then he heard a shriek. It was Laura.

She stood over him, hair flying. 'You have really gone too far, Scott,' she yelled. Neal, rushing up behind her, nodded vigorously in agreement.

48

Scott put little Hector down. 'I'm not finished yet,' protested the boy.

'Fax me a list,' Scott told him, taking Laura and Neal aside. He tried to explain what was going on. It wasn't easy, since he wasn't too sure himself.

'This isn't what you think,' he said. 'The kids just came up to me.'

'Look at you!' gasped Laura. 'Your hair! Your weight!'

Neal nodded. 'I think you're taking this Santa thing to an unhealthy level,' he said.

'This is really starting to scare me,' added Laura.

'Scare you?' asked Scott. 'So I've put on a few pounds and my hair's grey – big deal! Dr Meyers says I'm fine –'

'I never thought you'd stoop to changing your physical appearance to make Charlie like you,' Laura interrupted. 'You have no idea of how dangerous this is to a little boy.'

Once again Neal nodded in agreement. Scott could practically see him making a spiral with his index finger – the 'he's cuckoo' sign. Not that Neal had to. His opinion of Scott was written all over his face.

Scott didn't like where this was leading. His stomach did an Olympic-force flip. 'Dangerous?' he said. 'Whoa, now, wait a minute –'

Charlie ran over, and the three adults fell silent. 'What's wrong?' he asked.

'We're going home,' said Laura, taking hold of his arm.

Charlie pulled away, looking pleadingly at his dad. 'But the game just started.'

Laura took hold of him again. 'We're going home,' she repeated firmly. Halfway to the car she turned and called, 'You'd better get your act together, Scott . . .'

'. . . or else,' finished Neal.

Scott just stood there. He was so worried he couldn't even snap back at Neal.

He was still standing there when a little boy walked up. 'Hey, Santa!' the boy said. 'What's your fax number?'

Chapter Eight

A few months later, Scott stood in the bathroom getting ready to shave. As he'd explained to Dr Meyers, his normal razor wasn't working anymore – he'd shave in the morning and his beard would be full again by afternoon. So yesterday Scott bought an expensive new European model – sleek and black with three sets of shiny silver blades. 'It's the best we have,' the salesman had said. Scott hoped so. It cost as much as a television.

He lathered his face and began to shave. The new razor disposed of his entire beard in just under two minutes. This is more like it! thought Scott, admiring his face in the mirror.

The doorbell rang.

Scott hurried downstairs. The postman was waiting outside. 'Delivery for S.C.,' he said. 'You S.C.?'

'Scott Calvin, that's me. Who's it from?'

'No return address,' said the postman. 'I'll get your packages. There's quite a few.'

'Just leave them in the hallway,' said Scott. He

hurried upstairs, eager to see himself clean shaven again.

He looked in the mirror.

'NO!' It was a half-scream, half-gasp of astonishment. But it didn't change what Scott saw in the mirror – a roly-poly man with rosy cheeks, a full white beard, and a head of snowy white hair. The man in the mirror was –

The front door slammed, reminding Scott about the postman and the packages. He ran downstairs to find his hallway filled to the ceiling with cardboard boxes. A note was taped to one of them. 'Here's the list,' it said. 'Check it. Twice! Yours, B.'

Scott opened the first box. It was filled with a thick sheaf of paper covered with names in alphabetical order – children's names.

Scott looked up and saw his reflection in the hallway mirror – a roly-poly man with rosy cheeks, a full white beard, and a head of snowy white hair, holding a list of names. The man in the mirror was –

'NO!' This time it came out as a whimper. There's been a mistake, thought Scott. A postal error! The postman must have come to the wrong address.

He ran outside, but the post office van was at the end of the street and moving fast. 'Hey, you! Come back here!' yelled Scott. But the van kept right on going.

Scott stood there in his red silk bathrobe. He was covered with goose bumps. They weren't from the wind, cooler now that summer was ending. They were from sheer, downright perplexity. Who *was* he? He just didn't know anymore.

Charlie wasn't confused about who his father was. He was Santa, no question. Charlie also understood he had to keep that a secret. So when his mum offered to take him camping that weekend, Charlie answered carefully.

'I can't,' he said. 'I'm going to be with Dad.'

Laura was surprised. 'You can skip this weekend,' she said. 'He probably wouldn't mind. Unless you had something special planned.'

'We're cleaning out his garage,' said Charlie. He didn't tell her why. She wouldn't understand about all the cardboard boxes filled with the gigantic list – Santa's list – sitting in his dad's hallway. The boxes had to be put away in the garage before anyone saw them. They were part of the secret, too.

'Wait a minute!' said Laura. 'Are you telling me you'd rather clean out your father's garage than go camping?'

'Yup.'

Laura looked at her son. 'Charlie, you used to hate going to your dad's house. What's changed?'

'Dad,' said Charlie. 'He's different now.'

'I know!' said Laura, rolling her eyes.

'Good,' said Charlie. 'Then you understand.' And that was all he would say, no matter what his mum asked him.

He had to keep the secret.

It was much harder at school.

Charlie found that out one day in October.

He was at his desk after recess, looking for the glass ball Bernard had given him. He'd put it in his rucksack that morning. But now it wasn't there.

He searched his bag again, fighting a sick feeling in his stomach. The glass ball meant a lot to him. He couldn't have lost it!

'Looking for this?' Bobby Turrell tapped him on the shoulder with the glass ball, then snatched it away when Charlie grabbed for it.

'Hey!' said Charlie. 'Give that to me!'

Bobby was good at being the class bully. He taunted Charlie with the ball, waving it just out of his reach and smirking. 'What's the big deal with this thing anyway?' he sneered. 'It's just a stupid paperweight.'

'I promised I'd take care of it,' said Charlie.

'Promised who? *Bernard*?' mocked Bobby.

One part of Charlie wondered why Bobby liked making him miserable. Another part just wanted to beat him up. 'Give me the ball, okay?' He tried not to sound like he was pleading.

Bobby laughed. 'No wa–ay,' he sang. 'I'm gonna keep it. And you better not say anything, elf boy.'

By now the other kids were coming in from break. Then Ms Daniels came in and told everyone to sit down.

Charlie sat. He knew he couldn't say anything to his teacher. He had to keep the secret.

It wasn't easy being the son of Santa.

Charlie might have cheered up, though, if he'd been with Scott later that week.

Scott was having a good time. His day at B and R started with a pleasant surprise. A group of kids had been called in to test the Total Tank, and they hated it. So Mr Whittle was actually apologizing to Scott. This was a first. It was fun.

'You were right,' Mr Whittle told him, looking embarrassed. 'And I'm sorry I lost my temper with you. The kids do hate the Tank, Scott. I . . . uh . . . I'm hoping that with some design changes, maybe some of the things you suggested, we could reissue it next year. What do you think?'

Scott's eyes twinkled. 'Actually, Mr Whittle, I don't know if I'll be here next year,' he said. 'I might have to leave B and R.'

'Leave! You mean you have a better offer somewhere else?' Mr Whittle sounded slightly alarmed.

Scott had been right about the Total Tank. He could be right about other things. B and R needed him.

'Not exactly,' said Scott. 'It just looks as if ... as if I might have to distribute some toys soon.'

'Sounds like another job to me,' said Mr Whittle. 'Local outfit?'

'Up north.'

'What are they offering you, Calvin? I'll – I'll match it!' Now that Scott was actually quitting, Mr Whittle didn't want him to go. 'What's the position?'

Scott's eyes twinkled a little more brightly. 'Santa Claus,' he said.

Mr Whittle swallowed. He opened his mouth but no words came out, so he rolled his desk chair as far away from Scott as it would go. He had never had to deal with an employee who had lost his mind before. It was frightening.

'You're fired,' he finally managed to say.

Once Scott actually admitted that he might be Santa, he found himself in a much better frame of mind. He stopped worrying about his weight, and his beard, and his hair. He stopped shaving. He began checking the Christmas list, which was now safely in his garage. And on this particular morning he was really looking forward to seeing Charlie.

They had made a date to choose a Hallowe'en pumpkin to carve together – just the two of them.

But by the time they got to the pumpkin field, Scott knew something was wrong. Charlie was hardly talking. He wouldn't say anything about school. And his eyes were sad.

Scott sat down on a pumpkin in the middle of the field and took Charlie's hand. 'You okay?' he asked.

'Yeah,' Charlie mumbled, eyes down. He was a terrible liar.

'What is it, Charlie? Tell me,' said Scott.

For a minute Charlie didn't say anything. Then he sat down on a pumpkin next to his father. 'There's this kid,' he began, 'in school. He took something of mine.' He looked at Scott. 'He took that glass ball Bernard gave me.'

Charlie waited for his father to say, 'There's no glass ball. There's no Bernard. I'm not Santa. It was all a dream.' His stomach tightened up. He couldn't stand to hear those words.

He didn't. All Scott said was, 'Go on.'

'I told him to give it back. He wouldn't.'

'Did you tell your teacher?'

Charlie shook his head no.

'Why not?'

'Our secret, Dad,' said Charlie. 'You made me promise never to talk about North Pole stuff.

Ever. And he'll kill me if I rat on him. He's big. Real big.'

'Bigger than me?' asked Scott.

'Dad,' said Charlie, '*no one's* bigger than you.'

Later, as they carved a wonderful frightening face into their pumpkin, Scott continued their conversation. 'Charlie, why is that glass ball so important to you?'

Charlie hoped his dad would understand. 'Because . . . because of the magic,' he said.

'The magic,' repeated Scott. He smiled. 'You believe in that magic, don't you?'

'More than anything,' said Charlie.

'Charlie,' said Scott, 'if you believe in it so much, then you have to do something. Even if it means telling the secret.'

'But I can't tell!' said Charlie. 'You said –'

'I was wrong,' Scott said firmly. 'I shouldn't have made you keep that secret. I was trying to make things easier for me. But all I did was make them harder for you.'

'That's okay,' Charlie said quickly.

'No. I don't ever want you to be afraid to stand up for something you believe in, Sport. That's much more important than keeping secrets. But if this kid is *really* that big . . . maybe I –'

'Dad! Don't you think I can do it myself?'

'Sport,' said Scott, 'I believe you can do just about anything you set your mind to. Anything.'

Now it was Charlie's turn to smile. 'You *are* Santa, aren't you, Dad?'

Scott put his arm around his son. 'When it comes right down to it,' he said, 'it doesn't matter whether I am or not. But the way we're talking? That matters. *That's* important.'

And Charlie knew he meant it.

Chapter Nine

Not long after that, on a crisp November afternoon, Scott strolled through the neighbourhood, enjoying the sunshine and thinking about his list. He'd got more than halfway through it, and he was pleased at how many kids had been good this year. He wondered if the list was longer than usual and decided to ask Bernard when he got back to the North Pole.

Scott turned a corner and saw a burly man who was trying to open up the back of his pick-up truck while holding a large box. Scott stopped to help him, taking the box so the man could use both hands on the truck.

As Scott took the box, he realized it was a Total Tank. At the same time, he saw a boy about Charlie's age sitting in the truck. It was Bobby Turrell. Bobby the Bully.

An impish smile passed over Scott's face. 'Total Tank, huh?' he said to Bobby. 'Good luck.'

Bobby scowled at Scott. Then he recognized him. 'Hey!' he said. 'You're Charlie's dad.'

'Hi, Bobby,' said Scott casually. Then he snapped his fingers as if he'd just remembered something. 'Whoa! Bobby Turrell!' he exclaimed. 'You've been one *very* naughty boy this year, haven't you?'

Bobby looked surprised, then sullen. 'I didn't do nothing,' he muttered.

Mr Turrell came over. 'What're you talking about?' he asked, taking the box back from Scott.

'I don't know,' said Scott. 'It's the weirdest thing. It just came to me out of the blue.' And he walked off.

'What was that all about?' demanded Mr Turrell.

Bobby fumed. He'd get Charlie for this, the little rat fink!

Bobby found Charlie the next day, in the computer room. Charlie was working on a computer drawing of a sleigh and eight reindeer when Bobby yanked him out of his seat and into the hallway.

'What's wrong?' asked Charlie. Bobby looked even more scary than usual.

'You told! You told your dad it was me.' Bobby loomed over Charlie clenching and unclenching his fists.

'Did not,' said Charlie, standing his ground.

'He practically attacked me on the street, gave

me all this stuff about being naughty. How'd he know if you didn't tell?'

'He must have been reading the list,' said Charlie.

'What list?'

'The "who's been naughty and nice" list,' Charlie said patiently.

Bobby looked confused. 'Your dad has a list?'

'Of course he does,' said Charlie. 'He's Santa Claus!'

That did it. Bobby threw Charlie down on the floor and crouched over him. 'THERE IS NO SANTA CLAUS! Say it!'

'No,' said Charlie, trying to get up.

'Say it!' Bobby pushed him down again, harder this time.

'NO!' Charlie tried to struggle up, and Bobby punched him. Charlie backed off on his knees and slowly made it to his feet, breathing hard. His nose was bleeding.

This time Bobby hit Charlie hard in the chest with both hands, knocking him backward. 'There is no Santa!' he insisted. 'THERE IS NO SANTA!'

Charlie was panting too hard to speak, but they both knew he wasn't going to quit. 'Yes, there is,' he finally managed to gasp.

Suddenly a voice came from the top of the stairs. 'Yes, there is,' it said.

'Yes, there is,' said another voice from down the hall.

Bobby and Charlie looked up – and saw that a group of kids had come out of the computer room. 'Yes, there is,' said LaWanda. She was the biggest girl in their class, and her voice rang like a bell in the hallway. A murmur of agreement came from the others, who joined her to stand behind Charlie.

Bobby's eyes darted to the Exit door at the end of the hall. *He's afraid!* thought Charlie. All of a sudden he felt great.

'Give me my ball,' he said to Bobby.

Bobby stared at him. 'You want your ball?' he sneered. 'Your precious glass ball? Sure! I'll give it to you.' He went to his locker and pulled it out. 'In a million pieces, dork!' And he threw the ball toward the Exit as hard as he could.

Charlie watched numbly as the ball sailed through the air. How could he ever have expected to win against Bobby Turrell? How? He closed his eyes as if he could keep from hearing the glass ball shatter. Suddenly, in his mind, he saw his dad's face, smiling at him. 'I believe you can do whatever you set your mind to, Sport,' he heard his dad say, and Charlie's heart lifted.

After that it was simple. Keeping his eyes closed, Charlie pictured the glass ball as he'd first seen it, pulsing with magical light. Come back! he thought. Come back! Please!

The hallway was so quiet you could hear the wall clock ticking. Charlie opened his eyes and looked up. The glass ball hovered near the ceiling, glowing. Then it floated down into his hand like some giant jewel.

'Whoa . . .' A soft, awestruck murmur came from all the kids in the hallway.

Charlie's hands closed around the ball. It flickered once, as if greeting him, and went dark.

He smiled at Bobby. 'Thanks,' he said, getting up and leading the other kids back into the computer room. Life was good sometimes.

Charlie was still in an excellent mood when he got home from school, but he had a hard time explaining why to his mum. For some reason the blood on his shirt really upset her. And when he told her about the fight and how great it was, she didn't understand at all. She kept asking him boring questions, like how he had got into a fight in the first place.

'Well,' he said, 'Bobby Turrell said I told Dad about taking the ball. But I didn't tell Dad *who* took it. All the other kids were with me − they hate Bobby. Anyway, Dad saw Bobby on his own and told him he was in big trouble.'

'Trouble for what?' asked his mum. 'And who's Bobby?'

Sometimes his mother amazed him. Who's

Bobby? As if she'd never heard of him before! 'Aren't you listening?' he asked.

'I'm trying,' she answered. 'By the way, how did your father know about all this?'

''Cause he's Santa,' said Charlie matter-of-factly. Then he realized he was hungry. 'What's for dinner?' he asked.

His mother's response totally baffled Charlie. 'I'm going to kill Scott!' she announced.

Mums, he thought. You just can't work them out.

If Charlie had known what was on his mother's mind, his good mood would have popped like a balloon. In fact, Laura was furious with Scott. He had obviously been telling Charlie even more crazy Santa Claus stories, even though he'd promised not to. Now Charlie was so confused he was having strange fantasies and turning violent! She and Neal had to do something – and quickly.

They were in court the very next morning. They would let a judge decide if Scott's craziness was harming Charlie. It was the only way.

But when the judge asked to speak with Charlie alone in his chambers, Laura began to worry. Maybe she and Neal shouldn't have brought the problem to court. After all, Scott did love Charlie a lot. She sighed.

'Do you really think we should go through with

this?' she asked Neal. 'Taking away Scott's visitation rights is awfully harsh.'

'It's for the best,' Neal told her. 'Charlie's still talking about what happened last Christmas. 'That's not healthy or normal. He should be beyond the Santa Claus thing by now.' He took Laura's hand. 'I mean, come on, don't you remember when you stopped believing in Santa?'

'I do,' said Laura softly. 'I was around Charlie's age. I wrote Santa a letter every single week that year. All I wanted was a Mystery Date Game – remember those? – they don't even make them anymore.

'Well, anyway, Christmas came, and I got dozens of presents. Everything you can imagine. Everything but a Mystery Date Game. That's when I stopped believing.'

'Exactly!' said Neal. 'I was three when it happened. All I wanted was an Ovaltine Decoder Ring. But when Christmas came, no ring. That's when *I* stopped believing.'

Laura stared at him. 'You were *three*?'

At that moment Scott came bursting into the courtroom. His beard was full and snowy, and he wore a red sports jacket trimmed with white. He looked like Santa dressed for a cocktail party.

'Where's Charlie?' he demanded. 'I want to talk to him.'

'He's in with the judge,' said Laura.

Just then Charlie and the judge came back into the courtroom. Charlie ran up to Scott.

'It's all okay, Dad,' Charlie said to his father. 'I told him everything.'

Scott saw the expression on the judge's face. It was grim. That's what I was afraid of, he thought.

'My chambers,' ordered the judge. Once Scott, Laura, and Neal were inside, he looked at Scott gravely. 'Mr Calvin,' he announced, 'I've reviewed everyone's testimony and come to a decision. I don't like to do this during the holidays, but in the best interest of the child I must. I am granting the petition of Dr and Mrs Miller. As of today, your visitation rights are suspended.'

Scott had never felt so terrible in his life. How could they take his son away from him?

But they had. Slowly, Scott walked out of the courtroom to tell Charlie the news.

Chapter Ten

Scott was not giving thanks this Thanksgiving. He was crying.

He stood in the snow outside Neal and Laura's house, feeling miserable. He could see Charlie sitting at the dining table inside, and he looked miserable, too. He wasn't eating, just staring at the glass ball Bernard had given him. Scott sniffled. Life was terrible sometimes.

'Time to go.' Without even looking down, Scott knew who it was. Bernard.

'I can't,' he said.

'What's wrong?' asked the elf.

'I'm supposed to be Santa, right?'

'That's the general plan, yes,' said Bernard.

'And being Santa means making children happy?' Scott shook his head. 'How can I make other children happy when I've broken my own son's heart?'

Bernard looked up at him. 'You've got two choices,' he said. 'You can stand out here feeling sorry for yourself, failing millions of kids and single-handedly killing off the Christmas spirit. Or you can go into that house and deal with the problem and then come with me.'

For such a little man you are very smart, thought Scott. Then he headed for the front door.

There was a turkey on the table big enough to feed Charlie's entire class, but only three places were set: for Charlie, for Neal, and for Laura. Charlie knew his mum had been cooking for days, and everything looked great, but he didn't have much of an appetite. He missed his dad.

His dad must have been missing him, too, because as soon as Charlie said grace – 'Thank you for the food we are about to receive. Bless Mom, Neal . . . and bless Dad, too' – the doorbell rang.

And there was his father, right in their front hallway. Charlie was worried at first because Neal got angry with Scott for coming. He even tried to get him to leave, but Scott stopped him. Charlie had never seen his dad take charge like this – it was awesome!

Then Neal asked Scott if he still believed he was Santa.

'I don't know,' said Scott.

Charlie was astonished. 'What do you mean you don't know?' he asked his dad. 'Of course you are! Think of all those kids –'

'The only kid I'm thinking about is you,' said Scott.

'Dad, I'm fine,' said Charlie. 'But you can't let all those other kids down. They believe in you.'

Neal whirled around. 'Charlie, listen –,' he began.

'No!' said Charlie. 'YOU listen. You think you know him. You don't.'

'Honey, you're confused,' said Laura.

Charlie looked at her. 'Mom,' he said. 'I know exactly who he is. He's Santa. We were at the North Pole together. I saw it. The elves are real old, even though they look like me. And reindeer can fly and smile. Right, Dad?'

Charlie tossed the glass ball to his father, who fumbled for it and caught it.

'Believing is seeing. Remember, Dad?' Charlie asked.

Believing is seeing? Judy the elf had said that, back at the North Pole, thought Scott. What was Charlie trying to tell him? Scott looked at the glass ball and saw that it was pulsing with light, glowing like some giant jewel. His eyes widened. He laughed. It *was* magic!

Laura and Neal stared at him blankly. Scott realized that they couldn't see that the ball was glowing. To them it was just a silly plastic toy.

He walked over to Charlie and kissed him on the cheek. 'Could I just have a minute alone with my son?' he asked. 'You know, to say good-bye properly?'

Neal and Laura nodded and said they'd wait in the dining room. When they were out of earshot, Charlie and Scott hugged. 'Dad!' said Charlie. 'You saw it, didn't you? You saw the ball come to life!'

'You bet I did,' said Scott. 'How'd you get it back?'

'Like you said – I had to believe. And it worked!' said Charlie. 'It worked!'

Scott hugged Charlie again. 'Look, Sport,' he said. 'Bernard's waiting for me. I've got to go.'

'I'm coming, too, aren't I?' asked Charlie.

'I don't know' said Scott. He glanced in the direction of the dining room, where Laura and Neal waited. 'Maybe you'd better stay here with your mom.'

'Dad!' said Charlie. 'I want to be with *you*.'

'Oh, Sport,' said Scott. 'You don't know how many times I've wanted to hear you say that.'

'So you mean I can go?'

Scott hesitated. Then a grumpy voice said, 'So make up your mind, already!' It was Bernard.

Charlie was really glad to see him. 'Can I go, Bernard?' he pleaded. 'Please, can I go?'

'It's okay with me, Sport,' said the elf. They turned to Scott, who threw up his hands with a grin. 'How can I say no?' he asked.

And they were out of there.

Chapter Eleven

'It's nice to be back,' said Scott. And it was. The weather at the Pole was clear and sunny The elves were in high spirits. The production lines looked ready for the big Christmas push. And Judy's cocoa was even more delicious the second time around.

As he strolled towards the Workshop, Scott felt a surge of pride. The halls were lined with hundreds of photos and paintings of past Santas, and now he, Scott, was one of them. It was a great feeling.

'Soon I'll have my picture up there,' he said to Bernard and Charlie. 'I'm . . . I'm so honoured.'

But something was bothering Charlie. 'Bernard?' he asked, looking up at the pictures. 'How come there have been so many Santas?'

'That's . . . a good question,' Bernard said slowly. 'The best answer I can give you is . . . they suffer from professional burnout.'

'You mean because the job is so demanding?' asked Scott.

'No,' said Bernard. 'I mean a lot of people keep fires burning in their fireplaces, and some Santas . . .'

'. . . suffer burnout.' Scott finished the sentence with Bernard. He felt a little sick.

'Then there are overprotective homeowners.' Bernard continued. 'Santas get shot at. And, of course, quite a few Santas have gotten sucked into the exhaust of a DC-10. Oh, and storms are a real problem . . .'

'Hey!' said Charlie. 'Deal's off! No way! I'd rather have a live father than a dead —' He couldn't bring himself to finish. 'Look, Bernard,' he went on. 'You're sending my dad out on a pretty dangerous mission. He'll need protection. You've got to bring this place into the twenty-first century. You need computers! Stealth technology!'

Bernard looked sceptical. 'I don't know, Charlie,' he said. 'All that stuff sounds complicated. And expensive.'

'I thought you said you guys were magical!' said Charlie indignantly.

'Magical!' scoffed the elf. 'You think hot chocolate grows on trees? And you know what it costs to feed those reindeer? Comet eats like a horse!'

'Please, Bernard,' Charlie pleaded.

The elf sighed. 'I'll see what I can do.'

This sure beats the meetings at B and R, thought

Scott as he was led into the Research and Development wing of Santa's Workshop the next day. Everyone was a lot more cheerful, for example. No yelling, no arguing, no table slamming. Just a lot of busy little elves, working hard to make life safe for him – the new Santa!

He found out quickly that they were doing a great job. Led by an elf called Quintin, and helped by Charlie, they'd come up with all kinds of amazing new safety devices. There was a Santa hat equipped with a two-way radio. There were radar-jamming jingle bells and a snow-screen attachment for the sleigh, which could now rise straight into the air like a rocket. As Quintin and Charlie showed him what they'd been doing, Scott found himself feeling better – and safer – every minute.

But it wasn't until he saw the modifications to his Santa costume that Scott began to get really excited. The new suit was a technical marvel. It looked fantastic, as if NASA, Calvin Klein, and Harley-Davidson had designed it together. It was fireproof and bulletproof, so Scott didn't have to worry about getting shot. Best of all, it came with special removable pom-poms. When thrown, the pom-poms released a non-toxic gas that soothed people and put them to sleep – instantly. They woke up happy, and with absolutely no memory of Santa.

'Use the pom-poms when someone spots you,'

Quintin told Scott. 'When they wake up they'll think they were dreaming.'

Scott beamed. He could hardly wait to take off.

Back in his home town, there were people who couldn't wait for Scott, either. There were the children, of course. But also Neal and Laura. And the police.

Neal and Laura were certain that Scott had visited them on Thanksgiving to kidnap Charlie, and all they could think about was getting him back. They had had a phone call from Charlie, saying that he was safe – and then something about the North Pole and new technology. It only made them more convinced that their son was in the company of a madman. A dangerous madman. So they had been working closely with the police.

Neal had visited the station and talked to everyone there about Scott. 'He'll come to us on Christmas Eve,' he told them. 'We've got to be ready.'

So at the same time Scott and Charlie were taking off in the new attack-proof sleigh, a special heavily armed police squad was surrounding Neal and Laura's house.

And while Scott and Charlie enjoyed a cup of cocoa in the sky above the North Pole, the police were arresting every unfortunate person in the neighbourhood who happened to be dressed up as

75

Santa. They got seven in two hours. But none of them was Scott.

'He's not here,' said Laura, who had been called to the station to see the Santa line-up. She fought back tears. Where *was* Charlie? This Christmas was a disaster.

'This Christmas is the best,' Charlie told Scott happily. Everything was perfect – the sleigh felt like an airborne Ferrari, the reindeer were acting like pussycats, and he was even helping his dad navigate. It was awesome.

Suddenly Charlie realized where they were. 'Look, Dad,' he said. 'There's Mom and Neal's house! Let's go there next. I made something for them at the Workshop.'

'Sure,' said Scott. 'I have something for them, too.'

They headed down quickly, eager to leave their gifts under Neal and Laura's tree.

It turned out to be a big mistake.

The minute Scott got to the tree in the darkened living room, the lights came on and someone barked, 'Freeze!' Then three policemen, guns drawn, closed in on Scott and handcuffed him. There was no time for him to throw a pom-pom, no way to call for help on his radio hat.

In spite of all his precautions, Santa Claus had been arrested.

Charlie, watching from the roof, was horrified. So were the neighbourhood children. Attracted to their windows by the police sirens, they cried and shouted as Scott was forced into a patrol car. But their protests did no good. As Scott was driven away to the police station, a streetful of bewildered, sobbing children tried to make sense out of what they had witnessed. Santa arrested? How was it possible?

Back at the Pole, the elf named Larry burst into the control room. 'We've got a problem,' he said. 'Santa was at the Millers' and he's not responding.'

Quintin snapped to attention. 'All right, Bernard, let's see how good your new security is,' he said. Then he gave the order.

'Deploy E.L.F.S.!'

Instantly the crack rescue team that had been training for just this kind of emergency – four elves, dressed in jumpsuits, bristling with elf-size lethal weapons – strode out. They were E.L.F.S., the Effective Liberating Force Squad, and they were as eager to attack as terriers sniffing out a rabbit. They linked arms, activated their jet packs, and flew off into the night.

Half an hour later they were on Charlie's roof, reporting for duty.

Their leader helped Charlie on with an official E.L.F.S. jacket. 'Thanks,' Charlie said solemnly, zipping it up. There was so much riding on this mission – the happiness of childrenkind! The future of Christmas! It was a big responsibility!

As his jet pack lifted him into the air, Charlie smiled. It was also an adventure he'd been waiting for all his life.

'Let's go save Santa!' he cried.

Chapter Twelve

Desk Sergeant Chuzzlewit didn't mind working on Christmas Eve. He liked a nice quiet shift, and absolutely nothing was happening at the station tonight. That was fine with him. It was restful.

Not a creature is stirring, he told himself with sleepy amusement. He yawned.

Then he heard a voice. He peered over the edge of his desk. A gang of little kids dressed in shiny jumpsuits and rucksacks stood there staring up at him.

'We're looking for Santa Claus,' said one.

'Go home, kids,' said the sergeant. 'Visiting hours are over.'

'We're not kids. And we're not visiting,' said another.

'We came here to bust out my dad,' said a third. He was a little taller than the others, with larger features and a deeper voice. The sergeant peered at him. Had he seen that face before?

He checked the missing kid's photo on his desk. Yes!

'Hey!' he said, coming awake a little. 'You're the Calvin kid! Who are your friends?'

'We are your worst nightmare,' said one of them. 'Elves with an attitude.'

Before the sergeant could even wonder what the little fellow meant, the group had swarmed all over him, tied him up with ribbons, gagged him with a huge cone of candy-floss and run off to the cells.

I was wrong, thought Sergeant Chuzzlewit as a huge chunk of candy-floss melted in his mouth. Creatures *are* stirring.

His friend Officer Charles found that out next. He was on duty near the holding cell when he heard a noise and ran in to investigate.

Officer Charles had been on the force for almost thirty years, so nothing much surprised him anymore. But when he saw four tiny men and a young boy in the cell with prisoner Calvin, his mouth fell open.

'What the . . .?!' he began. Before he could finish they were all over him. In a matter of seconds his mouth was full of candy-floss and his arms and legs were immobilized, courtesy of many brightly coloured ribbons.

And there was more. Officer Charles watched in amazement as one of the tiny men pulled some tinsel from the Christmas tree in the cell and began sawing the bars with it. He blinked with disbelief as the tinsel cut through the bars as if they were made of plasticine, not steel.

'Tinsel,' said the E.L.F.S. leader. 'It's not just for decoration.'

The officer groaned in frustration as the entire party – Scott Calvin, the boy, and the four tiny men – cheered, ran out of the cell, and escaped into the night.

After wishing him a very merry Christmas, of course.

As the E.L.F.S. headed back to the Pole, elated with the success of their mission, Scott and Charlie made their way to Neal and Laura's house. They had gifts to deliver, after all.

Neal answered the door. He looked overwhelmed with relief to see Charlie. 'Thank heavens!' he cried, hugging him. 'Are you all right?'

'I'm fine,' said Charlie. He handed Neal the gift he'd made for him up at the Pole. 'I just wanted to give you this.'

A siren wailed in the distance. Police! Scott and Charlie looked at each other. 'I don't have much time,' said Scott as the siren drew closer.

'We can go now,' Charlie told him. He was eager to get back to the sleigh. They had a lot more work to do tonight.

'No!' It was Laura, fighting back tears of relief now that she knew Charlie was safe. She hugged him as if she'd never let him go.

Charlie didn't want to hurt her feelings, but after a minute he had to pull away, He turned to his father as if to say, 'Ready?'

Scott cleared his throat. 'Ah . . . actually, Sport,' he said, 'I'm thinking that maybe it would be better . . . if . . . you stayed here with your mom.'

Charlie couldn't believe his ears. Neither could Laura. 'What!' they exclaimed together.

'Dad!' said Charlie. 'I want to be with *you*!'

'And I want to be with you,' said Scott. 'But I can't have you with me all the time – that would be too selfish, Son. How about if you stay here during the year, and next year, around Christmastime, we get together again?'

Now Charlie was fighting back tears. 'I'll miss you too much!' he managed to say.

'I know.' Scott's voice was very soft now. 'But here's the thing – and this is a tough one.' He knelt down so they were face-to-face.

'There are a lot – millions – of children who are counting on me. Who believe in me. I can't let them down, Sport. I have a lot of work to do.'

Charlie knew what his father was trying to say. 'So I can't be selfish, either,' he finished for him. He knew his dad was right. But it was still hard getting the words out.

Scott gave Charlie a look full of love and tenderness. 'Listen to me,' Scott said. 'You have given me a wonderful gift. You believed in me when no one else did. You helped make me Santa! Selfish? You're the least selfish person I know.'

They hugged fiercely. 'I love you, Santa,' Charlie whispered in his father's ear.

'I love you, too,' his father whispered back. Then he stood to face Laura.

'So what do you say, Laura?' he asked. 'Charlie spends the year with you, but on Christmas Eve he comes with me. Is that all right?'

Laura looked at Scott. She had the uncanny feeling that she was seeing him – really seeing him – for the very first time. She found herself grinning. 'I can't believe it,' she stammered. 'It really *is* you. You're Santa Claus!'

Scott's eyes twinkled. 'It's something, isn't it?' he beamed.

A siren sounded again, much closer this time. Scott turned toward the door.

'Wait!' cried Laura. 'Don't leave yet!' She ran into the study and returned seconds later carrying a thick legal document.

'This is my Christmas present to you,' she told Scott. 'The custody papers.' And then she ripped them up.

Now it was Scott's turn to blink back a tear. 'Thanks, Laura,' he said. 'Merry . . .' He couldn't finish.

'What's all this boo-hooin' about?' asked a familiar voice. It was Bernard, sounding as impatient and bossy as ever.

'Just saying good-bye,' Scott told him, his voice husky.

'What good-bye?' demanded the elf.

'I'm not gonna see my dad for a long time,' Charlie's voice was as sad as Scott's.

'You still got the glass ball?' Bernard asked him.

Charlie nodded yes.

'Just shake it whenever you want to be with your dad.'

'Really?' Charlie's eyes widened. That changed everything!

Bernard raised an eyebrow. 'Have I ever steered you wrong?'

Charlie grinned. They both knew the answer to that one.

Scott's take-off in his sleigh was pretty spectacular. As the entire neighbourhood watched, the reindeer leaped off the roof with the grace and precision of dancers. It was awe-inspiring. Even the police, who had finally arrived at Neal and Laura's house, got misty-eyed.

Then Scott gave a mighty 'HO, HO, HO!', the reindeer circled over Neal and Laura's house one last time, and three beautifully wrapped presents came down from the sky.

There was an Ovaltine Decoder Ring for Neal. The Mystery Date Game for Laura.

And a football for Charlie.

When he unwrapped it, Charlie missed his dad so badly that he panicked. How could he last a whole year without seeing his dad?

Then he remembered the glass ball.

He ran to his room and pulled it out of its hiding place in one of his football boots. He carried it down to the back porch, shook it, and felt a thrill of joy as the ball began to pulse and glow with magical light.

He peered up at the sky hopefully. There were stars like crystal ornaments, and a bright crescent moon. That was all.

Charlie stood there, willing his father to appear. But he didn't. Fighting disappointment, Charlie headed for the back door.

'You miss me already? What's it been? Ten minutes? I mean, give me a break!' The voice was cranky. The voice was Scott's.

Charlie whirled around. There was his dad! As Charlie ran to him, Scott stopped pretending to be annoyed and opened his arms wide. 'Want to go for a quick ride?' he asked.

'You bet!'

'Of course, it's up to your mother,' said Scott. Laura was standing in the doorway watching them.

Charlie looked at her pleadingly, 'Mom . . .'

'Get out of here, you two,' she said.

So they did.

NIGHTMARE BEFORE CHRISTMAS
Daphne Skinner

Under the orange disc of the moon in Hallowe'en Land the creatures of the night are busy. Jack Skellington is the king of this strange world, but lately he's grown tired of the same old frights. Then by chance he discovers Christmas Town. What a wonderful place, he thinks, and what a wonderful idea if Hallowe'en Land came to visit Christmas Town.

Scary, funny and touching, this is the novel based on the film Nightmare Before Christmas.

FREE WILLY 2 ™
Todd Strasser

Willy, the mighty orca, is now free to roam the oceans and Jesse, his friend, has settled into a new life with his foster parents. But for both of them new challenges and dangers loom, which they can only overcome together.

A massive oil spill threatens to trap Willy and his family in a cove. Jesse is on holiday near by and immediately realizes the orcas are in danger – not just from the oil, but also from the company that wants to put the whales back into captivity.

For Jesse and Willy this is to be the greatest adventure yet.

RICHIE RICH
*A novelization by Todd Strasser based on the
screenplay written by Tom S. Parker & Jim
Jennewein*

Twelve-year-old Richie Rich has everything
money can buy: a billion dollar estate, a private
butler, even his own fast-food restaurant! All
Richie wants is to fit in with the kids in the
neighbourhood. Unfortunately Peewee, Omar,
Gloria and Tony just laugh at him. After all,
whoever heard of someone playing baseball in a
suit?

But when a dishonest employee of Rich
Enterprises tries to take over the company, it's
up to Richie to save the day. He needs all the
help he can get, and Peewee, Gloria and the
gang get to see a whole new side of the boy
billionaire. Now Richie must find his parents,
protect his friends and save the family fortune!

Top: Goatfell, from Brodick
Bottom: Holy Island and Lamlash pier from Lamlash, Arran

Top: Mount Stuart, Bute
Bottom: Sunset over Kiloran Bay, Colonsay

Top: Looking east to the Paps of Jura from Beinn Eibhne, Colonsay
Bottom: Camping on the edge of The Strand, Colonsay

Top: The 'whisky brothers' from Germany at Ardbeg distillery, Islay
Bottom: Ardbeg distillery, Islay

Top: The finish line of the Paps of Jura Fell Race
Bottom: Tobermory seafront, Mull

Top: Pier at Galmisdale, Eigg, with stone pillar commemorating the island's independence in the foreground
Bottom: Bullough mausoleum and the Rum Cuillin

Magnus ascending the An Stac screes, Skye

Descending the An Stac screes, Skye, in mist

Top: A Barra-bound ferry leaves Oban
Bottom: The Virgin and Baby statue on Heaval, Barra

Gatliff Trust Berneray youth hostel, Berneray

Top: West Beach, Berneray
Bottom: Petra and Peter, round-the-world cyclists in Leverburgh, Harris

Standing Stones, Callanish, Lewis

Top: Summit of Conachair, Hirta

Bottom: Dùn, The Village and Village Bay from Conachair, Hirta

Top: The Village, Hirta
Bottom: Stac Lee

Boreray & Stac an Armin

Flooding on the campsite at Sligachan, Skye

my skull. I was hungry and thirsty, tired but unable to sleep. I thought of breakfast: sausage sandwiches and oozing ketchup, creamy scrambled eggs, sizzling, smoky bacon, rounds of toast dripping with butter, steaming mugs of tea. All I had was porridge, miserable porridge.

It was after 4am, not quite dawn, when I had finally made it home. The rain had begun on the three-mile walk to Cleadale and it had fallen incessantly since then. Now Eigg was sopping wet. Rum had vanished in a film of mist. I roused myself. I had to. As it was Sunday, the Am Laimhrig shop was due to open for only an hour at midday. I was about to begin the trudge to Galmisdale when a jeep pulled over, the driver offering me a lift. This process of lift-sharing seemed to be Eigg's effective form of public transport. By the time we had left Cleadale, four of us were sat in the rear of the pick-up: a man in his 50s who was collecting a kayak from an arriving ferry, he said, as if this was a perfectly normal thing to do, and two pretty Canadian students. They were WWOOFers, the pair announced proudly.

'Oh, right,' I said, feigning knowledge, then admitting my ignorance a few seconds later. WWOOFers is the acronym for the Willing Workers on Organic Farms organisation, apparently.

'Did you have a good time at the ceilidh?' one of the Canadians asked, giggling.

'Yes,' I answered hesitantly, 'I did. Or at least I think I did. Why?' I asked gingerly. Both girls now giggled. Their response indicated a worrying level of intoxication, for I had no recollection of the students. As far as I was concerned, this was our first meeting.

I sought refuge in the café, desperately trying to revive myself and avoid anyone else who may have seen me making a fool of myself. A bacon sandwich and tea were good, but they could never live up to my earlier fantasies.

I walked to the other side of the village bay, pitching my tent on grazing land close to a beach. A handful of tents occupied by party-goers remained, but Eigg was gradually emptying as people returned to the mainland for work on Monday morning. With the tent up and the sun now out, drying the canvas, I crawled inside and fell into a long, profound slumber, waking late in the afternoon. In the initial moments of being awake I did not know where I was or what I was doing. Nor did I feel much healthier. My entire body was stiff, my mouth was bitter and dry, my head still pounded.

I roused myself again, returning to Galmisdale and walking along wood-lined lanes and across sheep country to reach the lower slopes of An Sgurr. The boot marks of thousands of walkers have created a moorland track beneath the northern cliffs of the escarpment and a further path climbs steeply onto the summit ridge. Once on the prow, walkers must double back on themselves, moving east over bare rock, to attain the highest point, marked by a circular stone triangulation pillar. It was clear in Galmisdale, but An Sgurr was coated in a thin veil of cloud. There were occasional breaks, revealing glimpses of the north side of Eigg or Muck to the south. Then a battering-ram of a wind blasted the cloud apart in one clean motion, finally exposing the full extent of the cliff-fringed land I stood upon. Eigg, five miles long and three miles broad, was the size an island – a perfectly-formed island – should be, for from the zenith of An Sgurr I could see it all. Eigg was large enough to support a reasonably-sized population, to have a primary school, to boast land that can be farmed, to host hundreds of bird and plant species, but small enough for the community to know one another and for those islanders to have the true sense of being surrounded by sea – an awareness that can be lost on the larger islands of Islay, Mull or Skye.

I descended quickly, breaking into a trot across the moor, but rather than going back to camp directly, I made for Eigg's rocky south fringe, where I located the narrow entrance of Uamh Fhraing, the massacre cave, inside which all but one of the late-16th century inhabitants of Eigg were smoked to death.

Boswell recounts the mass execution in his journal, describing the carnage impassively: 'Young Coll told us he had been in the cave, and seen great quantities of bones in it; and he said one can still observe where families have died, as big bones and small, those of a man and wife and children, are found lying together.' The cave became a grim draw to later visitors. Sir Walter Scott, the novelist and poet, is said to have seen bones in the cave when he came to Eigg in 1815 and the geologist Hugh Miller identified the remains of family groups during his Hebridean tour aboard the *Betsey* in 1845. The bones were removed and buried some time after Miller's visit, but a skull of a child aged five or six was found by a holidaying boy in the cave in the 1970s.

The slaughter was committed by the MacLeods of Dunvegan, who were avenging the similarly brutal killing of their kinsman at the hands of the MacDonalds of Eigg. The sides had been adversaries for years when a MacLeod galley came to be moored off Eilean Chathastail, a little isle separated by a narrow channel from Eigg's south-east seaboard, in poor weather in 1577. As the group, led by a MacAskill and a foster son of Alastair Crotach, the chief of Dunvegan, feasted on cattle taken from the island, they were butchered by an Eigg force. The leaders were spared, but their fate was no better. With their arms and legs broken, they were set adrift on the open sea, apparently facing a slow, painful death. Only the tide carried their boat back to Skye. The MacLeods' response was swift. A force was despatched from Dunvegan to exact revenge. Seeing the enemy galleys coming, the people of Eigg made for Uamh Fhraing, their preferred place on the island to take refuge.

The MacLeods searched the island, finding only one person, an old woman living at Hulin, on the north of Eigg, who would not betray her people. The MacDonalds had been in the cave for three days when one of their number was sent out to see if the MacLeods had left. The invaders had abandoned their search, convinced the islanders had fled to another island, but as the galleys of the MacLeods rounded the south side of Eigg, the scout could clearly be seen against a white backdrop of freshly-fallen snow. It was a fatal mistake by the MacDonalds.

The MacLeods, led by Crotach, who vowed not to change his clothes until revenge had been exacted, and his son, Uilleam, traced the people of Eigg to the cave. They redirected a waterfall concealing the entrance, before stacking material that could be set alight outside the cave. A battle was impossible, for the mouth of the cave was too small to allow more than one person to pass through at a time, preventing a swift attack from either side. The Mac-Donalds' situation was worse, though. Were they to emerge from the cave, they would be easily slain one-by-one.

Uilleam said the hiders should be shown no mercy; Crotach was willing, however, to free the women and children. Undecided, Crotach called on God's will: If the wind was blowing away from the cave in six hours time, he would spare the islanders. The time elapsed and the wind blew towards the land, sealing the awful fate of the 398 MacDonalds huddled inside Uamh Fhraing. A single islander survived: the old woman of Hulin.

The cave had not been easy to find and I spent several minutes clambering over rocks still slippery from the receding tide until I found the boulder-strewn entrance. Jamie – a

MacDonald, though not a bitter one – had recommended I come here and step inside the cavern, which Boswell described as 'spacious and lofty like a church'. I hesitated at the entrance, peering into the gloom. I was plucking up the courage to enter when my phone rang, with the sudden shrillness that shattered the silence causing me such great surprise I abruptly reared up, dashing my head against an overhanging rock.

I approached the cave for a second time with an even greater sense of trepidation. There was a troubled, uneasy atmosphere in this place. Even the waves bumping the rocks seemed to be possessed with some menace. A cloud of soaring birds filled the air. Dusk was falling.

I imagined the possibilities of the cave's interior: bones, cobwebs, cold, bare rock, dripping water echoing in the darkness, a musty stench, startled, swooping bats. I conceived the horrors of being a prisoner in this dungeon, first for three consecutive days, then the realisation that escape was impossible, then the realisation that a fire was being set, and then the dreadfulness of knowing an awful death was near. I thought of the spirits that haunted these cliffs, forever mournful and restless, perhaps vengeful, slipping invisibly in and out of the cave. I could have cried for them had I not been so overcome with fear. I shivered and backed away, moving quickly over the greasy, seaweed-coated rocks and up a narrow track to the lip of the cliffs, and began running away from the cave as fast as I could.

11

Rum

On a good day, Rum appears majestic and heroic. On a bad day, it appears to have the largest, most vicious midge population in the northern hemisphere.

Lesley Riddoch

⊗

Pinned to a notice board in the visitor centre on Rum is a large black and white poster. It was the first item in the room to catch the eye. Above the words 'the Rum midge', a swarm of the insects, human-sized, their teeth poised and sharp, attack a group of terrified men, women and children. The mesh nets worn over their heads are futile, for the people are encircled by the enemy. Striking with fantastic speed, the midges show no mercy, no pity for their victims. There is no escape.

The dreadfulness of their plight is reminiscent of a scene from a horror movie. If only the poster was being ironic. If only this was fiction.

I camped, with well-founded trepidation, pitching my tent next to the shore of Loch Scresort. I would stay here for two nights. My fate depended on the elements. If the wind blew, there would be no midges. If the wind dropped, they would eat me alive. For now, surrounded by forest, mountain and sea – and silence – Rum was a marvellous, midge-free place to call home.

The campsite occupied a long, thin strip of grassland, the sea loch on one side, an undulating gravel road that connected the island's ferry pier and the hamlet of Kinloch, where all but one of the 40 human inhabitants of Rum lived, on the other. The plot was surprisingly well-equipped. Neat, wooden shelters packed with firewood – presumably to deter campers from venturing into the forest to hack their own – bookended the site. There were two hot-water showers and a block of toilets.

Taps delivering fresh water and basic trough sinks were dotted about the camping ground. The water, however, as on Eigg and Holy Island, came with a health warning. Environmental investigations by Highland Council had found the supply on Rum to be 'at risk from bacterial contamination, which could be harmful to health'. A decree pinned to the wall of my nearest shelter went on solemnly: 'Care should be taken not to swallow water while showering or bathing'. Even using the water to brush your teeth seemingly carried the risk of a lingering, painful death.

It is temptingly easy to be blasé about such warnings: adopting an it-will-never-happen-to-me outlook on life, bemoaning how even Rum is unable to escape the clutches of officious health and safety. Yet to assume that because this was Scotland and because this was the Hebrides, the land would be free of animal or human interference, or not riddled with chemicals, would be naive. The risk of contracting water-borne infections of the ilk of E. coli and Weil's disease are real and potentially fatal.

Even so, I chose to be blasé, ignoring the warning. I reread the council's pronouncement. The key word was 'could' – the water 'could' be harmful to health. That one word created an area of fuzzy grey, a glimmer of hope that illness or death post-consumption was in no way inevitable. I also had to consider the practicalities of my situation. I came to Rum with no water. I had no way of purifying what water there was on the island and nor did I have the inclination or patience to spend mind-numbing hours boiling water in my tiny cooking pot to make it drinkable. To reassure myself, I carried out a very simple experiment. Turning the tap on, I filled my pot to the brim and held up to the light for close investigation. Does the water look tolerable? Yes, I decided. Does it taste tolerable? Yes. It did not smell, nor was there anything untoward swimming about in the liquid (not that I could see with the naked eye, anyway). With my scientific trial concluded, I drank liberally.

The shelter had clearly seen happy times; a previous camper had used a marker pen to scrawl the steps for various Scottish dances, including the Gay Gordons, strip the willow, dashing white sergeant and the Canadian barn dance, on a strip of plywood. I imagined the wild nights of Rum campers: dancing and whisky, eating and singing, stoking a roaring fire, recklessly gulping the island's bacteria-infested water. While I was lost in my reverie, another camper, a man in his 60s, with a gnarled, tanned face and a northern English accent, arrived and began pitching his tent close to mine. He announced he had come to climb 't'hills and t'mountains'. He was an unlikely candidate to get the party started.

I had nothing to do: it was bliss. Sitting outside the village café, at first eating a cheese sandwich and drinking tea, then gazing absent-mindedly out to sea, I easily whiled away two hours. It was hot and still. Had I known I would never see a hot and still day in the Hebrides again, I would have savoured every second. Eventually I thought I had better do something, have something to show for the day. I wandered back to camp, where I pulled on shorts and trainers, before running away from the sea and into the uninhabited interior of the island. My pace was easy and unhurried as I followed the course of a rocky track that gradually ascended Kinloch Glen, the Kinloch River always to the north. After about two miles I reached a junction; I hesitated, wondering which path to follow. Going north, a track swept down Kilmory Glen, the location of a research project begun in 1953 on red deer, one of the longest-running studies of its kind anywhere in the world. Going west, trails broke off to either Bloodstone Hill, a towering peak of, funnily enough, bloodstone, overlooking the Sound of Canna, or a secluded bothy at Guirdil Bay.

Forgoing the options of north and west, I ventured south, continuing on a track bound for the one-time township of Harris. After passing a stationary jeep, the occupants of which were observing a black dot in the sky, I saw no other people. I had Rum to myself. From the crossroads, the roadway, dry and rocky, wound upwards to reach a pass beneath the slopes of 556-metre Ard Nev. Here I paused, turning to see the view behind. The stirring, stupendous sight of the cloudless Black Cuillin on Skye filled the vista to the north.

I continued towards Harris, captivated by the natural brilliance of Rum, taking bounding strides downhill. My shirt dangled from the waistband of my shorts, the sun warming my bare shoulders. The run was the most joyous of my life, so joyous it was effortless. Red deer flitted nervously across the distant moor, moving as a herd, stopping momentarily to gaze at me, before making graceful haste again. As I descended further, an astonishing view of a verdant Glen Harris was unsheathed, all the way to Atlantic Corrie below the mountain giants of Askival and Hallival. The Rum Cuillin was grander than it had appeared from Eigg or the sea to the east. Ahead was a brilliant blue sea, a white surf crashing against a rocky beach. I was surrounded by greatness.

Two houses still stood at Harris, one, a black house,

looked like it had been abandoned decades earlier, the other more recently. A short way beyond the end of the track was a mighty building of stone, resembling a Greek temple and curiously sited, for such structures are not typically built on grassy cliff tops overlooking the Atlantic and so far from civilisation. The roof, decorated by two crosses, was raised on the shoulders of great pillars, behind which were the stark, oblong shapes of three tombs. Stepping over a low chain fence, I approached the edifice, climbed three stone steps and passed between a pair of pillars. The tombs were half in sunlight, half in shadow. I leaned forward to touch one of the sarcophagi, but thought better of it. I was fleetingly afraid. I ran down the steps and away to a safe distance. I looked back at the tombs, guilty for my intrusion on this ethereal place.

The mausoleum was built by Sir George Bullough, a Lancashire manufacturer and laird of Rum for 48 years until his death in 1939. Sir George occupies one of the tombs; his father, John, and his wife, Monica, were laid to rest in the other two. Despite its grandeur, the mausoleum was not originally intended to be the family resting place. A vault, constructed on a hillside close by, with a lavish interior of Italian mosaic, was the predecessor to the mausoleum. But after a visitor likened the structure to a public toilet, the laird ordered it to be blown up. All that remains is part of a wall and a family coat of arms.

Turning my back to the mausoleum, I crossed a stream and then climbed away from the coast, passing through the collapsed walls of what would once have been a croft, to reach a plateau of grass. Stretching away to the east was Glen Harris, the land marked by the parallel ridges and furrows of lazy beds, where crops, including cereals and potatoes, would have been cultivated by the generations of Harris residents – a reminder that life had formerly thrived here. As with many of the other townships on Rum, hundreds of years of human existence at Harris ceased when people were cleared for sheep.

I could have come to Harris on an ugly day, one of lashing rain and furious gales. The mountains would have been mist-cloaked, the sky leaden, the sea angry and frothing. As it was today, Harris was the most extraordinary place I had ever set eyes on. Moments of sublime flawlessness are rare; such instances depend on the harmonious collision of mood, place and time. Today, now, somehow, the pieces fitted together: the command of the mountains, the roll of the sea, the shimmering brilliance of the sky, the adrenaline of exertion, the haunting emptiness of the land, the spectacle of Sir George's mausoleum, the calmness and liberation of thought. Nothing was out of place. I ran back to Kinloch in a state of wonderment.

My visit to Rum coincided with a weekly lecture on the island. I arrived early to find one other person in the community hall: my fellow camper, sitting cross-legged and scowling. 'How do?' he nodded. The hall was the hub of island life – a café, computer suite, library, meeting place, newsroom, party venue, rain shelter and tourist centre rolled into one. A ranger employed by Scottish Natural Heritage, the dominant landowner on Rum, came next, setting up a computer and projector, before waiting for more people to arrive. Three others appeared. The ranger sighed, accepted his gig was hopelessly small, and began, launching into a potted history of Rum.

People have eked out an existence on Rum since the Stone Age, making the island one of the earliest places of settlement in Scotland. Christianity came to Rum in the 7th and 8th centuries, with stone crosses found at Kilmory dating back to this period. The island was then ruled by the

Vikings, whose names of glens and mountains - Askival, Dibidil and Hallival - remain today, until the 13th century, when Rum became part of the Hebridean empire of the Lords of the Isles. The population peaked at more than 400 in the early 19th century, but that number was slashed to fewer than 150 following the Clearances in the 1820s. Some 300 people were shipped to Nova Scotia in Canada to begin new lives. The MacLeans of Coll, the then landowner, replaced the people with 8000 sheep. With sheep-farming proving uneconomical, the island was sold in 1845 to the Marquis of Salisbury, who set about turning Rum into a hunting and fishing estate. The Bullough era began in 1888, first under John, then from 1891, Sir George. The industrialist funded the construction of Kinloch Castle, made of red sandstone sourced from Arran, in the early years of the next century. The epoch ended in 1957, when Sir George's widow sold Rum, excluding the mausoleum, to the UK government, and the island was handed to the Nature Conservancy Council to manage.

Nature reserve status provided protection for deer, sea-eagles and the 60,000 pairs of manx shearwaters that live on Rum. Environmental and geological designations were sprinkled on Rum like confetti. The island became a biosphere reserve in 1976, a special protection area for birds in 1982 and a site of special scientific interest in 1987. But protection came at a public relations cost, for access by tourists was severely restricted, leading to Rum being dubbed 'the forbidden isle'. Times have changed, however. Scottish National Heritage had made a point of calling Rum 'the welcoming isle' in its literature.

Rum went down the community ownership trail blazed by Eigg when homes in Kinloch and surrounding land were taken over by residents in 2010. After centuries of laird dominance, the transfer was a quantum leap for Rum, but the ranger hinted that the long-term viability of island life hinged as much on community ownership as on the future of Kinloch Castle. The ornate building – the only accommodation provider on Rum – is badly deteriorating. A multimillion-pound renovation is required. The castle came close to receiving the badly-needed funds when in 2003 it featured on the BBC series *Restoration*.

Celebrity backer Arabella Weir stated the case: 'If Kinloch Castle is left, it will crumble and the people of Rum will lose out. If restored it would attract hundreds of visitors and Rum would become an active community with a massive injection of income. It is in the middle of this wild, remote Hebridean island and it is just too spectacular to let go.'

Perhaps the voting public thought the comedian was joking? The castle was only a runner-up. The cash – some £3million – agonisingly slipped through Rum's desperate fingers.

The castle needed a saviour. Prince Charles seemed to be that deliverer, visiting the island with the Duchess of Rothesay in 2006 to examine the state of the castle. The prince's call prompted understandable optimism. The cause was adopted by The Prince's Regeneration Trust and an £8million scheme for the castle's rejuvenation drafted. The plan spoke of conservation and repair, of a 30-bed hostel and self-contained apartments, of a café and bar. Yet the plans remain plans; money is the obstacle. Millions of pounds are simply hard to come by.

I made the acquaintance of the midges of Rum on my return to camp. It was mid-June, dusk and the air was still: midge o'clock. They were waiting for me, each carrying a baseball bat. With a miniscule wingspan of 1.4 millimetres, the Highland midge appears innocuous. But what midges lack in size, they make up for in quantity. And I had never seen such quantities as I would on Rum. The island is a veritable midge factory. In June, July and August, billions of the beasts pour forth from its numerous bogs and heaths. It is the females who wreak havoc, desperately seeking blood so they can reproduce. The males, meanwhile, are happy to leave humans alone, feasting on nectar or rotting plants instead.

The midges on the shore of Loch Scresort were lazy at first, flitting around my head but not biting. They had the courtesy to allow me to brush my teeth in relative peace. As I made a dash for my tent, they seemed to wake up, realising immediate action was required – or they would go to bed with empty stomachs. A black cloud pounced on me. The insufferable attack commenced. At least shelter – and escape – was very near. I wondered how long I could have endured, how long before I could bear the awful sensation no more. Just 10 seconds seemed too long. The midges would never get bored. Females can detect the carbon dioxide emitted by humans from a distance of 100 metres away. A swarm can deliver 3000 bites an hour. Never mind smoking the MacDonalds to death, the MacLeods of Dunvegan should have brought them to Rum and let the island's midges devour them.

I fumbled with the zip on the tent's outer sheet, the number of midges seemingly multiplying many times with every second I spent scrabbling. Diving into the narrow gap between the two sheets, I zipped up the outer and unzipped the inner, and frantically flung myself inside, finally snapping the last zip shut. I was safe. The midges could not get me in here. Not that they seemed to gather that. The insects surrounded the tent. Black specks crawled across the canvas, the beat of wings making a low, incessant whirring. They would be with me all night. Midges have been estimated to cost the Scottish economy £286 million in lost revenue every year. I was beginning to see why.

My tent was a graveyard of midges by dawn. Little black bodies were everywhere – coating the canvas, strewn across the items I had left between the inner and outer sheets and encasing a bottle of olive oil. Sweeping away the debris and binning the oil, I tried to convince myself tonight would be different.

I set out into the hills above Kinloch, climbing a steep track to reach a rocky pass between Barkeval and Hallival, two of Rum's Norse-named Cuillin. As I ascended, I met the northerner, who was descending.

'Couldn't be bothered,' he muttered ruefully as we passed.

He had started out at 4am with the bold intention of conquering the five highest hills of Rum: Askival, Ainshval, Hallival, Trollabhal and Sgùrr nan Gillean, ranging from 712 to 802 metres in height, but was returning to camp without even claiming one of the peaks. These mountains are what remain of a volcano that was once a 2000-metre high dome, but collapsed as pressure in the magma chamber dropped. The volcanic legacy of the Cuillin is a crumbly, peridotite soil, making high slopes prime bird-burrowing territory. Tens of thousands of pairs of manx shearwater breed on Rum – as many as one-third of the entire global population of the species. I saw my first burrows below the pass, with hundreds more appearing as I began a slow ascent of Hallival. Despite the colossal population, there were no birds at home. Manx shearwaters spend daylight hours feeding at sea, before returning to land under the cover of darkness to avoid predators.

An ominous pall of mist was rolling in from the west, shifting ever closer. One by one, the peaks of west Rum were engulfed, with Ainshval, Trollabhal and Sgùrr nan Gillean vanishing soon after. Askival and Hallival suc-cumbed a minute later. An outlook that had extended across Rum and Eigg only an hour earlier was now re-stricted to a hazy, 20-metre box of soil and rock. Like the northerner, my plan had been to climb all of the Rum Cuillin in a single day. In truth, I lacked the mettle for such a long expedition, and as frustrating as the mist was, it gave me the excuse I needed to cut short the outing.

Even so, I could not leave Askival, the highest point on the island, unclimbed, so I forged forward, passing over the summit of Hallival, and descending steeply to a bealach between the two mountains. A faint track crossed a narrow, grassy ridge, before a jumble of rocks blocked the way ahead, forcing me to skirt around the east side of Askival. A scramble between the rocks, following the occasional boot marks of other walkers, brought me to the zenith of the island. There was nothing to see, only a battered triangula-tion post. The clag seemed thicker than ever. It was not going to clear.

Abandoning any attempt to scale the entire ridge, yet unwilling to simply retrace my steps to Kinloch, I descended sharply to the south, setting a course for invisible Beinn nan Stac, a striking, pointy hill I had admired from the ferry to Rum. Away from the main route, Rum instantly became rougher and wilder. Grazing goats hurried away at the sight of me. The descent was uncomfortable: cliffs required care-ful down-climbing, hidden entrances of burrows waited to swallow my feet, while the grass was long and the gorse thick.

I emerged out of the mist to see my destination, some 250 vertical metres shorter than Askival, was mercifully clear. A short while later I was standing on the summit of Beinn nan Stac. The higher tops of Rum remained drenched in mist.

The drop to Glen Dibidil from my grassy pinnacle was perilously steep. Far below was a bothy, standing close to the Dibidil River and reputedly rat-infested, and the narrow line of a footpath running parallel to the coast. According to my map, this track stretched from ruined Papadil Lodge at the far south of Rum to Kinloch, and to avoid an exhausting trudge across miles of rough ground, it was a path I urgently had to meet.

The practicality of locating on the ground what was represented as a black, wiggly line on a map seemed uncomplicated. The path was no more than a mile away. My rationale was that if I aim for the coast, sooner or later I will inevitably reach the track. A mile? It was a meagre distance; men can run such a distance comfortably under four minutes. My mile was a wretched one. Even escaping the summit of Beinn nan Stac posed difficulties I had not bargained for. Dropping south to Glen Dibidil was out of the question, so I instead went north, slithering ungainly down a line of steep, slippery rocks. Passing over boggy, bumpy ground, overrun with gorse, I made for a stream draining the south-east slopes of Askival. I felt embarrassed at being here, for traipsing over this wild land. I knew Scottish National Heritage would resent my presence. There was a reason for there being no paths here.

Every step carried me closer to the sea but the track to Kinloch remained elusive. I came to a faint walkway traversing the hillside and followed the trail for some way, only for it frustratingly to peter out on a prow. I unfolded the map again. Was this the path? Perhaps it was merely a track carved by the feet of animals? I had clearly seen the route in Glen Dibidil, but that was near the bothy. Did it even exist here? I descended again, stopping at the edge of a muddled slope of grass, gorse and rocks. I could see the trail now – it was at the bottom of this daunting drop. I threw myself down, stumbling and tripping, pricking fingers, knocking my head against a boulder, ripping my trousers, clutching at plants to break my fall. At last, I hobbled gratefully onto the track. Making a mental note never to descend Beinn nan Stac in such fashion again, I commenced the long trudge to Kinloch.

The three-mile march, creased and undulating, sometimes dry, more often wet, was interminable. Dizzy with tiredness, I plodded on, rarely raising my eyes from the ground, fixating on the restorative powers of the café, or, if that was shut, the pub within Kinloch Castle. I longed for rest and respite, but with every step towards that reward a morbid dread grew in my mind; I knew what the evening would bring. My route veered inland, passing a tumbling waterfall, before rising for one final time to a brow, beyond which was the vision of Kinloch and Loch Scresort.

Dusk fell. It was time for round two: man versus midge, Goliath versus countless Davids. I underestimated my enemy, conceiving they could not be so violent for a second night. It was an error of judgement, an error I would pay for. I was cooking in the shelter when the midges found me, forcing me inside my tent to eat. Emerging five minutes later, I walked headfirst into a frantic, grey, droning crowd. They clung to me like prickly magnets. I ran to the sink, swilled out my pot, and relieved myself while walking backwards, a delicate and potentially messy task, but necessary. A stationary target is a dead man, and there is a place where no man wants to be bitten. I still had unfinished business, for I had to return to the shelter to retrieve cooking equipment, food and books, before I could seek the sanctuary of my tent again. I had now been outside for no longer than a minute. But it was too long. Earlier I had the foresight to put on repellent before the midges came out to play. It was useless. Hundreds of the beasts were clambering across my bare legs and arms, crawling through my hair.

Such was the desperation of my panic-stricken state, it did not occur to me to brush them off as I lunged into the tent. The reality of what I had done and what I could not undo was instantly apparent. My tent – what had been gloriously midge-free seconds earlier – was now swarming with my adversaries. I cursed the midges; I cursed myself.

The situation was grave. I was incredulous and infuriated at my idiocy. The midges could not believe their luck: a blood-rich quarry with no chance of escape. I contemplated abandoning the tent, letting the midges have it, and begging a bed at the hostel within Kinloch Castle. But that would mean admitting defeat. I fought back, commencing a process of mass slaughter. I assaulted them with whatever I could lay my hands on: books, maps, even clothes. At first it seemed hopeless, as if I was attempting to turn back the tide. What use is a map of the Small Isles against the brutal efficiency and the kamikaze tendencies of the Rum midge? I kept at it, slamming, slapping, swiping, smothering and squashing, every death a small victory.

Bodies were beginning to stack up. Fyodor Dostoeskvky could not have conceived a copy of Crime and Punishment would serve such a purpose. The pages were splattered with specks of black and red. The outer sheet was encircled by midges, like the previous night, only the buzzing was louder, as if they were offering a whining chorus of moral support to dying brothers and sisters inside. After 20 minutes I was satisfied. The counter-offensive had been a success. Outright victory was impossible. I could never defeat them all, but I had vanquished the greater part of their invading force. The rest – the afraid, the injured or the infirm – retreated to a corner, where they murmured angrily. Panting and sweating, I lay down my weapons. When I finally fell asleep, it was a slumber disturbed by haunting dreams of crawling bugs and flying insects.

Midges. There was little else to talk about.

'Never again. Rum? In June? Midge season? Never again, never ever again,' the northerner groaned as we waited by the pier for a ferry bound for Canna. He lifted up the legs of his trousers to show me the evidence: numerous dots where midges had struck.

I nodded in agreement. With the midges in this mood, life on Rum – even with its beauty and splendour, its coast and mountains, its history and wildlife – was scarcely worth living.

12

Canna

People may think it's boring to live here but actually it is quite fun. Just because there are only fourteen of us doesn't mean we can't have fun.

Canna Primary School website

Canna – four miles long and one-mile wide, the westernmost outlier of the Small Isles – wore a garland of mist. MV *Lochnevis* would pause here for two hours before returning first to Rum and then to Mallaig. The deadline gave little time for exploration. I would stay low since there was nothing to be gained from ascending Càrn a' Ghaill, the island's 210-metre, cliff-sided summit, such was the impenetrable quality of the shroud.

An unsurfaced road led away from the harbour and its graffiti-strewn rocks, passing through the strung-out township of A' Chill, to a road bridge link to Sanday, Canna's island neighbour. These gentle, green islands were home to 255 people in 1841. A harsh period of clearance followed, and today, the population numbered fewer than 20. It would be a tragedy if life on Canna and Sanday – inhabited since prehistoric times – were to go the way of the other once-populated, now empty, Hebridean isles. The two islands have no doctor or police; no mobile phone reception; no pub or shop (provisions must be purchased from the mainland); a primary school with a roll of four (up from one in 2006); no electricity between midnight and 6am.

Who would want to live here? Hundreds of people, it turns out.

The National Trust for Scotland, the manager and owner of Canna and Sanday, have been public in their desire to stem population decline, launching a series of appeals for families to relocate to the isles. Potential islanders should, however, possess an appropriate skill, the trust stressed – an ability to build, garden, join or plumb, or the wherewithal to run a café or bed and breakfast. Failing that, adults should be employed or self-employed (the island does, at least, enjoy broadband). And, perhaps most important of all, the incomers must be able to live harmoniously with the existing islanders.

One such appeal in 2006 garnered in excess of 350 responses, including interest from all over the world. The trust need not have cast its net so wide: the successful couple, who would run a guesthouse on Canna, hailed from Oban. More incomers followed in 2008, this time a family of four from Llanelli in South Wales, with the father given the task of restoring the jungle-like gardens of Canna House, the former home of John Lorne Campbell, a Gaelic folklorist and contemporary of Compton Mackenzie who gifted the islands to the trust in 1981.

I was mulling over the pluses and minuses of life on Canna, not that I could see much of it, when I heard a familiar voice behind me.

'Ey up lad.'

It was the northerner.

He had cheered up, the absence of midges on Canna the reason. 'There's no bogs 'ere, you see,' he explained.

We walked on in silence, leaving behind A' Chill and crossing the wooden bridge – rebuilt in 2006 after its destruction by waves – to Sanday. 'That's three islands I've been on today. Not bad at all,' my companion muttered, almost breaking into a smile. We walked as far as a shrine on the Sanday side of the bridge before turning back, retreating to Canna.

The northerner quickened his pace. He seemed convinced we would miss the ferry if we did not hurry. I let him go ahead and rather than proceeding to the harbour, I continued to the east coast, coming to the crumbling remains of An Coroghon, a hundreds-of-years-old castle and later a prison. The wife of a Clanranald chief was incarcerated here to prevent her from meeting her lover, a MacLeod from Skye. Rather than being built on the flat summit of a sea stack, the tiny fortification clings to a steep rock face looking inland. The structure inspired a verse in Sir Walter Scott's narrative poem published in 1815 *The Lord of the Isles*.

> Signal of Ronald's high command,
> A Beacon gleam'd o'er sea and land,
> From Canna's tower, that, steep and gray,
> Like falcon-nest o'erhangs the bay.
> Seek not the giddy crag to climb,
> To view the turret scathed by time;
> It is a task of doubt and fear
> To aught but goat or mountain-deer.

A sign erected by the trust at the foot of the stack warned visitors to 'keep well clear'. I ignored the notice, clambering uphill over extremely steep, loose ground, only to hurriedly think better of my forbidden expedition, using the excuse of an imminent ferry to catch as a reason to flee.

13

Skye

It seems as if Nature when she hurled The Cuillin up into the
light of the sun said: 'I will make mountains which shall be
the essence of all that can be terrible in mountains.'

W.V. Morton

୫

The Inaccessible Pinnacle sounds as if it should be an
unclimbed, unconquerable peak, rising majestically and
snow-capped in a far-flung corner of the Himalayas. The
fearfulness of the name invokes a vision of a sheer-sided,
soaring colossus of a mountain, cloaked with an aura of
invincibility. As Lyonesse is a mythical island in Arthurian
legend, the Inaccessible Pinnacle could easily be its mountain equivalent: the greatest, most exquisite summit of all,
forever remaining an unobtainable objective.

Alas, no. The Inaccessible Pinnacle – or the In Pinn as it is
commonly known – rises high on the jagged spine of the
Black Cuillin on Skye, the largest island of the Inner
Hebrides. Gigantic and grand, the In Pinn arouses equal
measures of horror and wonder, but it is not inaccessible.
Yet the name is not given in irony. The pinnacle is a vertical
pillar of basalt projecting from the south-east side of the
summit of Sgùrr Dearg, standing almost 1000 metres above
sea level. It is unquestionably the hardest of the 283 Munros
to climb, for it is the only such mountain that demands its
conquerors have the adroitness of a rock climber. One
mountaineering guidebook goes a step further, calling the

In Pinn 'the hardest mountain summit to attain in all of the British Isles'.

What makes an ascent of the In Pinn potentially terrifying is its exposure – the empty space beneath the climber's feet. In the case of the In Pinn, the exposure is, in places, hundreds and hundreds of metres. Should the climber put a foot in the wrong place, make a clumsy move or – heaven forbid – their equipment fails, the exposure is how far they could potentially fall. And climbers do not generally survive falls of hundreds and hundreds of metres. As Charles Pilkington, the Lake District cragsman who with his brother Lawrence made the first recorded ascent of the In Pinn in 1880, testified: 'A slip from the east end would be fatal.'

There are further complications. Firstly, to descend the In Pinn, summiteers must abseil from its highest point, down a sheer face of rock: thrilling for some, terrifying for others. Secondly, in a place where precise navigation is more crucial than on any other mountain range in the UK, the volcanic gabbro rock, the predominate constituent of the Black Cuillin, plays wicked tricks on compasses. The magnetic properties of the rocks distort readings, making compass bearings unreliable. And thirdly, with Skye being an island, the weather is governed by the sea, so mist and rain are the rule. If proof were needed, rain fell for more than 50 consecutive days, including all of August, on Skye in 2009, the island's longest uninterrupted spell of wet weather since 1861.

As the name evidently suggests, the In Pinn was once considered insurmountable. The assertion was made by Captain Wood, a British Admiralty surveyor, who mapped the south Cuillin in 1859, identifying a 986-metre summit – the In Pinn – as being unconquerable. He was, of course, proved wrong by the Pilkington brothers 21 years later and then by successful ascents of the harder, steeper west ridge in 1886. Yet the In Pinn was never mastered by Sir Hugh Munro, with his several attempts foiled by bad weather. The pinnacle was not regarded as a Munro in his original tables (documenting Scottish mountains considered to be higher than 914 metres) published in 1891. The author instead listed Sgùrr Dearg, which stands eight metres lower than the In Pinn (but is far more accessible), as the superior mountain, with the In Pinn relegated to its subsidiary. The oversight was corrected in 1921 when the In Pinn was rightfully elevated to Munro status.

One factor convinced me that I, a novice climber, could master the In Pinn: a dog had done it, in fact, several dogs. Hamish Brown is thought to have been the first person to climb not just the In Pinn, but all the Munros, with his Shetland sheepdogs, Kitchy and Storm, at his heels. Peter Sinclair, a retired police officer from Inverness, and his boxer dog, Kerry, did likewise, completing a round of the Munros in 2009. Describing their ascent of the In Pinn to the *Herald*, Sinclair said: 'I was climbing on one rope and Kerry was on the other in a harness being pulled up by a friend. She was docile throughout. If she had shown any sort of distress at any point I would have stopped. There were some moments when I thought, why are we doing this? and I'm sure she thought it too.'

So there, if a dog had reached the summit of the In Pinn, surely so could I?

Like Kerry, I could not overcome the In Pinn alone, so I called upon the services of a climber, Magnus, an Inverness fisherman who counts base jumping and skydiving among his interests. Compared to throwing himself out of a plane, the In Pinn would be a cinch, the least of Magnus's worries. He promised to get me up the pinnacle, provided I could successfully guide us to the foot of the column. Once on the rock, he would be my lifeline.

Three nights before the assigned day, the weather forecast for Skye was flawless: clear skies and light winds. It was too good to be true, too fortuitous. And so it turned out. By the eve of the climb, the forecast was an utter contrast: drizzle, mist and only the slimmest chance of the summits being cloud-free. Magnus called. It was Saturday night and he was at a party; I could hear animated chatter in the background. Immediately, I sensed reluctance from the tone of his voice. The forecast was too bad, he said. No wind though, I countered. It would be foolhardy to attempt the In Pinn in mist, especially when neither of us had climbed in the Black Cuillin before, he responded. Why not tackle it on a fine day, when we could appreciate the climb, appreciate the view – undoubtedly one of the finest, most dramatic of any in the islands – from the top? And if the In Pinn was wet, it would live up to its name – it would be inaccessible. He was right, of course. I told him so, but pressed on Magnus my determination to carry on regardless, to at least give the climb a go. After all, when would we both be free again on the same day? This might be our only opportunity.

I was beginning to obsess. The In Pinn was only a lump of rock. It was not going to go away; it would still be there next week. If the weather was worse than forecast when we arrived, then we would re-evaluate, I bargained. Magnus said he would think about it, and hung up. It was his decision. He was the climber. I needed him more than he needed me. I braced myself for disappointment.

Magnus rang back 20 minutes later, his mind made up, the tone in his voice altered: the In Pinn was on.

We motored west from the Highland capital, the subject of the In Pinn unmentioned in conversation until after we had crossed the bridge over Loch Alsh to Skye. The weather was getting progressively worse. Loch Ness had been bathed in sunshine and only the occasional cloud tufts were obscuring the highest mountains of Glen Shiel, but the Red Cuillin – the gentler, lower hills of Skye – were drenched in a forbidding, grey mist. The forecast was spot on. Celebrated romantically as the Misty Isle, Skye was living up to its reputation for inclemency.

Leaving Kyleakin we finally broached the knotty matter of the In Pinn. There are two ways to climb the pinnacle, either by its sloping east ridge, rated as a moderate climb, or by its vertical west ridge, a VDiff standard rock climb. I had assumed we would attack the east ridge: the easy, sensible option in light of the weather. But Magnus's attitude was that if we were going to travel for the best part of three hours from Inverness and walk two miles to the foot of the In Pinn, with the extra weight of climbing equipment on our backs, then we were going to do it 'properly'. And that meant the hard way. His boldness unsettled me, heightening my nervous state. I had never climbed outdoors. Nor had I climbed indoors for three years, and then at a basic level. I had always thought of climbing as awkward and cumbersome, preferring to run or walk over the hills, carrying the lightest weight possible.

We swept along the coastal road, flashing through Broadford and Dunan, Magnus concentrating on the road ahead, while I fixed my eyes on the islands of Raasay – where a delighted James Boswell once danced a jig on the highest point, Dun Caan – and Scalpay to the north. The enormous bulk of Glamaig, its head decapitated by mist, appeared as the road turned to run parallel with Loch Ainort. At Sligachan we followed the minor road to Merkadale, where a single-track route forked south-east over a small pass before plunging into Glen Brittle. There is a magnificent spectacle of the western edge of the Black Cuillin – the sort of place that would inspire artists and poets – from the glen, but not today. Mist hunkered low on the mountains, resting on the 400-metre contour, some 600 metres beneath the summits.

We pulled up outside the Glen Brittle Memorial Hut, an 18 bunk hostel used by clubs and individuals affiliated to the British Mountaineering Council or Mountaineering Council of Scotland. A little further up the road was one of two bases used by the Skye Mountain Rescue Team. The team were called out on 36 occasions in 2009, from reports of rivers in spate and stumbles, to overdue climbers and falls of rock, involving 1700 voluntary man hours. Three people lost their lives on the Black Cuillin that year: two on Am Basteir, a 934-metre fin of rock, its name apparently meaning the executioner, although there is no such word in Gaelic, and the third while descending Sgùrr nan Gillean to Glen Sligachan. Another climber suffered severe injuries, including a fractured pelvis and a punctured lung, in a 30-metre fall from Sgùrr nan Eag.

The In Pinn is similarly no stranger to accident and incident. In 2008 a man dislocated a shoulder after falling during an attempted solo climb of the pinnacle. Then in 2009 a woman climbing the west ridge slipped and fell onto the east side of the In Pinn, sustaining arm and head injuries. Interestingly, Kerry and her master were also among those to receive emergency assistance on the Black Cuillin in 2009, after he became disorientated in mist on Sgùrr Dubh Mòr. Sinclair's wife raised the alarm when he failed to ring home. The headline in the *Scottish Sun*? Mutt' n rescue.

The base was manned, for members were carrying out a training exercise in the mountains. One of the team members and Magnus spoke for several minutes, their language sprinkled with the jargon of rock-climbing: abseil points, camming devices, pitons, screwgate caribiners and slings.

Whatever was discussed, he seemed persuaded that Magnus, the climber, was competent enough to get me, the non-climber, safely up the In Pinn.

We set off with renewed confidence, soon passing the dozen on-exercise mountain rescue team members, and ascended a gentle slope above a waterfall. Ignoring a path that leads to the foot of the knife-edge western approach to Sgùrr Dearg, we proceeded along the glen towards Coire Lagan, with the view south stretching across sea to Canna, Eigg and Rum. The vista was short-lived, for we ascended inexorably into mist: a dark, mysterious world of jumbled shapes and shadows.

Magnus and I were a curious pairing, today in particular. Hilary and Tenzing, or Herzog and Lachenal, we were not.

Less than 24 hours earlier I had been taking part in the Highland Cross, an annual 50-mile running and cycling race between Kintail and Beauly. I had exceeded all my expectations, finishing 10th out of the 688 finishers and covering the course – split into a 20 mile run and a 30 mile cycle – in a shade over four hours. It had been a gruelling journey. At the changeover point in Glen Affric I was verging on the delirious. The run had been hot and exhausting. I scarcely knew what day it was. Hearing someone bellow my number, I went scampering after a marshal to retrieve my cycle. I tugged off a trainer in a furious haste, without bothering to untie the laces. My entire right leg cramped. The marshal grabbed my rancid, reeking foot and stretched my throbbing leg to try and ease the pain. Another marshal issued slow, deliberate instructions: 'Take your vest off. Put your shirt on. Put your helmet on.'

Once on the bicycle, cramp became my nemesis. The slightest change of motion – a flick of the gears, even a sideways glance or repositioning on the saddle – would trigger shuddering pain. It was bearable and fleeting until I reached the outskirts of Cannich, a third of the way into the ride. There, a wave of cramp engulfed my limbs, like bullets being fired into my calves, syringes being inserted into my quadriceps. The muscles twitched horribly, an ugly sight. I could no longer turn the pedals, with my speed dropping until it was so slow I was on the cusp of falling sideways. I had to make an urgent decision. Either I fall – or I pedal. I pedalled, extremely slowly at first, howling with pain, swearing uncontrollably over and over again, legs trembling, gradually generating a little momentum. It sounded as if I was being tortured. Slowly, the anguish ebbed away, yet the episode shook me mentally and physically. The torment had been so abrupt, so fierce. I dreaded its return. Cramp came as sporadically as it had on the approach to Cannich, returning with vengeance only once – on the finish line. Crying with pain again, I was gently lifted from the saddle by two marshals and a paramedic and carried to a waiting ambulance.

Magnus had also completed a Highland Cross, not yesterday, but two years earlier. His achievement was purely in covering the distance. So determined was he not to stop that he kept moving forward even as he vomited with exhaustion. Born with a heart defect, Magnus's childhood and adolescence had been punctuated by long stints in hospitals, with the longest of all lasting twelve weeks. At one point, his odds of survival plummeted to one in three.

As an adult, Magnus was fighting fit, training meticulously on his road cycle and walking extensively in the Highlands. Standing 6 feet tall, with an athletic build, and rarely seen without a smile on his face, Magnus's demeanour gave no hint of his malfunctioning heart. But his is an existence of uncertainty. In late May, three weeks before our In Pinn escapade, Magnus had been three miles into the running leg of the Nairnshire Challenge, another north of Scotland duathlon, when he sensed a problem, a life-threatening problem. His pulse had rocketed, spiralling to a sky-high 234 beats per minute, an impossible figure for a 'normal' adult. Pluck or idiocy, call it what you will, but Magnus continued. Fellow competitors – now overtaking him in droves – offered him energy drinks and water. He politely pointed out that they were unlikely to solve the problem. A hospital was what he needed, and quickly.

Since what Magnus described as a 'bitter disappointment' to put it mildly (he could have died, again), he had cycled on only two occasions. The stumbling block was confidence, not fitness. So climbing the In Pinn was either courageous or plain daft, depending on a person's outlook on life. Were Magnus to ask his specialist whether he should attempt a mountain walk involving almost 1000 metres of ascent, followed by a strenuous climb of the In Pinn, he knew what the answer would be. Hence he did not ask.

What Magnus had not told me before we set off from Glen Brittle was that he had suffered an even more recent heart scare, just two nights previously. 'Chronic chest pains,' he told me later, sounding non-plused, making chronic chest pains sound like a stomach ache. 'It turned out to be just an abdominal hernia.'

If Magnus was struggling, he did not let on. Nor did I not feel the need to enquire after his welfare. I trusted him to tell me if there was a problem. And if there was, well, I would probably panic. We gained the loch in the upper reaches of Coire Lagan, following a path that became ever fainter and ever steeper. I had been here before, with Fi several years earlier. It was the furthest I had ever ventured into the Black Cuillin. It was a pity the mist had blanketed the mountains for I knew the view from here was tremendous; the outline of the Western Isles would have been visible on the horizon.

The loch itself sits in the bowl of an amphitheatrical corrie encircled by jagged, thrusting peaks, their flanks strewn with chutes of loose rocks. Alpine in appearance, Coire Lagan was likened by the mountaineer and writer W. H. Murray to 'the courtyard of a giant's castle'.

A traverse of the summits around the corrie ring – Sgùrr Alasdair, Sgùrr Thearlaich, then tackling either Collie's Ledge or King's Chimney, both rock climbs, to reach Sgùrr Mhic Choinnich and Sgùrr Dearg – is a technical and potentially perilous enterprise, which demands a head for heights. A superior trial still is a traverse of the entire Black Cuillin ridge, arguably the greatest mountaineering challenge in Britain. The traverse – from the top of the most northerly mountain, Sgùrr nan Gillean, to the southernmost, Sgùrr nan Eag, or vice-versa – is only seven miles long. But the traverse requires long, arduous ascents and descents to get onto the first mountain and off the last, visits 18 distinct tops, 11 of which are Munros, climbs a total of 3000 metres and can only be attempted by a fearless rock climber and scrambler. The record is an astonishing three hours and 17 minutes, set in 2007 by mountaineer and runner Es Tressider, who described the experience as 'like running in heaven'. Mere mortals can only marvel at his time, yet it is still a laudable achievement to cross the ridge in two days, with a midway bivouac along the route. Our efforts seemed paltry in comparison. I wondered if Kerry had completed the traverse, or Kitchy and Storm. A canine with a name like Storm sounded like he could do it solo and with only a bone for nourishment.

The veil of mist meant we could see very little, with visibility extending no more than 10 metres across the loch. We ate lunch silently, neither of us willing to discuss how the thickness of the shroud would affect our ability to navigate to the In Pinn, let alone climbing it.

At last I asked the question that had to be asked: 'Are you prepared to continue?'

'Yes,' Magnus simply returned.

We had briefly resumed our progress when we heard voices echoing across Coire Lagan. We followed the sound, soon coming to a guide and his client, who were laid flat out on rocks after descending the Great Stone Shoot, a name very accurately describing the terrain to Sgùrr Alasdair, the 992-metre highest point of the entire Black Cuillin and Skye. As Brits do – even on mountains – we exchanged futile words about the weather, and pressed on. Our destination lay on the opposite side of Coire Lagan, up what are known as the An Stac screes, which stretched 200 metres above our heads.

Ascending scree does not list highly in the hobbies of many people, even the hardiest of mountain climbers. Murray described the ascent of the Great Stone Shoot as 'drudgery beyond compare'. The An Stac screes were no better. The catchphrase, two steps forward, one step back, can literally be applied to the process. Every step dislodged rocks, which then rolled under our boots, making progress frustratingly slow. I longed for a firm surface. For half an hour I was back on the Paps of Jura, as rocks catapulted off my ankles. Magnus and I followed parallel courses, for the one below would have been showered by mini-avalanches triggered by the leader's movements had we walked in single-file. Our clothes and hands were caked in dust and mud. Our world had shrunk to contain only this miserable scree slope. We could see nothing else. Eerie echoes in the mist occasionally reached our ears: the distant rumble of tumbling boulders or phantom-like voices. Each time we would stop dead, look at one another, listening hard, hear nothing more, then continue. At last the gradient eased and we came to a ridge, the one linking Sgùrr Alasdair and Sgùrr

Dearg, I assumed, which dropped very steeply to the east. It was not where we wanted to be.

'This isn't the right place,' I murmured. Magnus nodded in affirmation, and we shuffled along a faint path that skirted the An Stac buttress beneath the In Pinn.

We walked on, almost on auto-pilot; the mist obscuring the hideous drops I knew now surrounded us. We gradually worked our way around the buttress, reaching the west ridge of Sgùrr Dearg, where the terrain changed from scree to a series of awkward rock slabs, made slippery by the moisture in the air. The In Pinn arrived without warning, its great outline towering above us, vast and brooding in the grey cloak. It was imposing, tremendous; it made me shake with fear and exhilaration. I wanted to climb it desperately, but I also wanted to run away from it. As the hill-walking author Cameron McNeish surmised: 'A narrowing blade of rock leaning against the summit crest of Sgùrr Dearg, this impressive feature will either delight you, or scare the pants off you.'

Despite the conversation in the car, there was an unspoken understanding, I thought, that we would climb the easier, east ridge of the In Pinn.

'Let's just have a look at the west ridge,' Magnus suggested, 'as we're here.' I dumbly agreed, leading us over slabby ground to the opposite side of the pinnacle. I touched the In Pinn for the first time, caressing the rock as if it was a religious icon. I was not daunted by it. It looked climbable. Even as a non-climber I could make out the obvious handholds. Another conversation about which ridge to climb was not needed. It was to be the west.

We prepared. Harnesses were put on, straps tightened, knots tied. Magnus gave me a crash course in belaying. VDiff obviously stands for very difficult, which is confusing to anyone unfamiliar with climbing because the words infer such an ascent would be fraught with danger. But climbing terms were coined decades ago when a VDiff was indeed very difficult. With the equipment and innumerable guidebooks climbers now have at their disposal, a VDiff is no longer a very difficult climb, although it is not easy either. Climbs are graded not simply on their steepness, but on a host of other factors, including the extent and number of holds for feet and hands, as well as exposure. The 20-metre long west ridge of the In Pinn may not be technically taxing, but the exposure elevated it to a VDiff.

Magnus would ascend first, inserting gear into the rock as he gained height, thus making him safe lest he fall. By this method, known as trad or traditional climbing, he was the leader, the one who would take the risks; I was the second. Attaching himself to the rope, he handed me the other end.

'If I shout 'slack', let the rope out. Or 'tight', bring it in,' he said. 'Don't be offended if I shout at you,' were his parting words as he began climbing.

'Remember I've never climbed outdoors,' I said to his back. Magnus either did not hear or chose to ignore my blurted statement.

He eased up the wall, effortlessly covering two or three metres in a blink of the eye. Then he came to a juddering halt, uncertain of his next move. He had put no safety equipment in the wall yet. If he fell now, I would be unable to hold him. He would be hurt very badly. I tried to push such thoughts to the back of the mind and I craned my head upwards, watching him anxiously. At last he managed to force gear, a block attached to a metal wire, into a crevice, then pulled on the wire until it jammed into the wall. Even from the ground I could see his tense and stiff frame instantly relax. He was now on the trickiest part of the ridge, negotiating a tight corner to reach a crack in the rock.

Another piece of gear went in and he swiftly vanished from view, disappearing into the unknown. He shouted down to me to let the rope out. I heard nothing for a moment, and then a cry of exultation: 'I'm up.'

It was my turn. Drizzle had started to fall. Unlike the rough gabbro that makes up much of the Black Cuillin, the pinnacle is formed of basalt, a rock which becomes slippery when moist. My hands felt cold and numb. Suddenly the wall had acquired a fresh veneer of grandeur, while the holds, so blatant a short time ago, had shrunk to miniscule proportions or disappeared altogether. My assurance faltered.

'Climbing,' I shouted, but it would be another minute before I summoned the courage to place my feet on the rock of the In Pinn. After half a dozen haphazard swings, I had two hands and two feet on rock. I was poised on a horizontal ledge, a narrow lip scarcely a metre above the ground. Even that seemed a long way. I was going nowhere. My prospects seemed hopeless. I was hideously out of my depth. I cannot do this, I decided. My arms ached; my legs were drained of energy. For the first time, the excuse of Highland Cross weariness entered my mind, a mind surging with self-doubt. The east ridge was my escape route. If I cannot do the west, I can scramble up the east, I convinced myself. I would still have gained the In Pinn.

It was the wrong way to think.

'I'm going down,' I shouted huffily, 'let the rope out.'

'Watch out. I'm going to throw my climbing shoes down,' Magnus called out, tossing the boots to the foot of the pinnacle.

They were at least two sizes too small but I prised my feet into them, hoping they would give me a slight advantage, even if it was psychological only.

'Climbing,' I yelled again. This time I brought my feet

onto the ledge in one smooth movement. Once there, I did not hover, I did not procrastinate. The rope was holding me. There was nothing to fear, I told myself. I hauled myself upwards, trending left as Magnus had done. It was ungainly and unpretty, but it was effective. I was climbing, reaching the first nut in a wave of ecstasy. I removed it, clipped the caribiner to the loop on my harness and continued, now to the right. My fingers felt around the corner, joyfully finding the crack in the rock. I wiggled up the groove, bellowing, 'tight, tight, tight,' to Magnus. Once above the crack, the ground was no longer vertical. I could see the summit, the giant, vertical boulders marking the highest point. It was within touching distance. I felt like I was running, my feet scarcely brushing the ground. I looked back briefly to see the lip of Sgùrr Dearg now a long way below, rising like a wave about to break on the glen. Then I was standing next to Magnus – wearing only socks on his feet – breathing hard, grinning delightedly, the indecision, the nervousness of the previous minutes gone forever. I was Bonington, Cool and Hillary rolled into one, the greatest climber that ever lived. Or at least that is how it felt.

I had conquered the Inaccessible Pinnacle.

14

Barra

It always rains on tents. Rainstorms will travel thousands of miles, against prevailing winds for the opportunity to rain on a tent.

Dave Barry

❧

'Looks like rain.' I was crouched over my tent, pulling taut the canvas, pushing pegs into soft ground. Leaving the pier, I had sauntered east along the deserted streets of Castlebay. Having already spied a place to camp from the deck of the ship that brought me to Barra, I followed a single-track lane, passing a cluster of homes, before the road became a track across grazing land. I continued until I found what I was looking for. On the eastern shore of Castle Bay, over-looking one of the four islands around the coast of Barra named Orosay, I made camp.

A colossus of a man, belly protruding over belt and a grey beard turning white, was standing over me. I followed his gaze across the bay. The water was flat and grey, the sky cloudless. The horizon was clear, not a storm cloud in sight. He shook his head knowingly. 'Are you sure?' I asked sceptically. I waited, anticipating a nugget of Barra wisdom: because the cattle have turned their horns to the south-west; because whales are swimming clockwise laps of the island; because cats are barking and dogs are mewing.

'It said so on the weather forecast.'

The ferry journey from Oban to Barra, across the Sea of

the Hebrides, took seven hours – time enough to fly between London and New York, across the Atlantic Ocean. The voyage had entered its fourth hour when, having expired all indoor diversions, I stepped outside, surveying the horizon from a wind-blasted deck. The once blank canvas of sea was filled with a new vision. A wondrous chain of islands had appeared on the western prospect: the Outer Hebrides. I ran my eyes across their dark, grey outlines, starting in the south, finishing in the north, un-ravelling the jumbled shapes one by one: the linear, the lofty, the lowly and the lumpy. The lands of Berneray, Mingulay, Pabbay and Sandray, forming the tail of the Western Isles, jostled for attention, and then came Vatersay, an island linked to Barra by a causeway since 1991. The campaign for a land bridge between the two islands was inadvertently fuelled five years earlier after the drowning of a bull named Bernie. The animal was being pulled across the narrow strait separating Barra and Vatersay in the wake of a rowing boat when he perished.

The largest and loftiest island so far, Barra, a place of sandy strands and striking scenery, stood peerlessly above the rest. Immediately north came Eriskay, an island roman-tically linked to its near-neighbour by a tale of whisky. In February 1941, a US-bound steamship, SS *Politician*, carry-ing a cargo of 264,000 bottles of whisky, foundered on rocks off the islet of Calvay in the Sound of Eriskay. Cases were rescued and taken ashore by the people of Barra and the Uists, who drank the amber nectar a little too freely, so freely that several islanders were hauled before the courts and jailed.

The story inspired Compton Mackenzie's novel *Whisky Galore*, who began his book with a tongue in cheek reference to the infamous episode.

'By a strange coincidence the SS *Cabinet Minister* was

wrecked off Little Today two years after the SS *Politician* with a similar cargo was wrecked off Eriskay; but the coincidence stops there, for the rest is pure fiction,' he wrote.

A film, *Whisky Galore!* followed in 1948, with Ealing Studios choosing Barra as the backdrop for the fictional Little Todday. A plaque on the Royal Bank of Scotland building in Castlebay, the principal town of Barra, pays tribute to the film's director, Alexander Mackendrick.

A line of fearsome hills and one mountain – Beinn Mhòr, the zenith of the southern half of the Western Isles – dominated the east coast of South Uist, concealing the miles of gently-sweeping meadows of machair adorning the west coast. Further north, but indiscernible as separate islands, were low-lying Benbecula, little Grimsay and North Uist. Over the Sound of Harris was Harris itself, seen from the Sea of the Hebrides as a confusion of cliffs and mountains.

My world was now these islands, the isles of the Outer Hebrides. The vanishing mountains of Rum and the fading profile of Skye were the only reminders of the Inner Hebrides. I had arrived at nowheresville.

I was awakened by an otter. Or, as I gathered my thoughts in the immediate, confused moments after the severing of sleep, an otter is what I imagined must be the cause of the disturbance. The prospect of such a creature rousing me from slumber was not as illogical as it seems, for according to the bringer of bad weather tidings, I was camped in otter territory. Previous campers had been known to unzip their tent in the morning to find such an inquisitive creature staring back, he said.

I lay very still and silent, listening to the repetitive, gnawing-like sound, as if something was trying to chew its way into my tent.

It had to be an otter. I was honoured by my night-time visitor, renowned for its elusive nature. I had never seen one in the wild. But as welcome as the otter was, I did not want it ruining my tent; another five minutes and we could be sharing a sleeping bag. Carefully unzipping both sheets, I gently swung my legs onto the grass and pulled myself out, then tiptoed around the tent. My presence had not deterred the creature. The sound had continued unabated. This was one determined otter.

There was no otter: only the wind flexing an over-tensioned strip of elastic, causing a noise reminiscent of chewing. Mine was still an otter-less existence.

I glanced across the bay. It was dark. Darkness was unusual. Even when I went to bed as late as midnight, I had rarely seen darkness, true, black darkness when a hand before a face is not visible. A half-light (or half-dark, depending on one's outlook on life) seemed to last for hours, sometimes all night. On midsummer's day in Barra in 2010, the sun rose at about 4.40am and set at 10.30pm, meaning there was little more than six hours of night-time. Dawn broke at a similar time over London, but the sunset arrived an hour earlier. The influence of latitude is even more marked the further north one travels in the UK. There were just five hours of darkness on midsummer's day for the inhabitants of Unst, one of the northernmost islands of Shetland, where the sun rose at 3.30am.

Deprived of it for so long, I had a new appreciation for darkness. I sat outside the tent door, listening to the night, the silence of the night. I could hear my heart beat, my shallow breath. The moon was a white smudge in the sky, partly obscured by cloud. Were it midwinter I would have seen more stars than I could ever count, but in this semi-darkness I could see none. The hills on the western side of Castle Bay and Heaval to the north were silhouetted against the sky. The orange lights of Castlebay and the white bulbs of a cruise liner berthed in the bay twinkled serenely. A red light on the opposite side of the village flickered like a noiseless siren. Darkness and the illuminations of darkness were forgotten treasures.

Built on an islet plinth in Castle Bay, Kisimul is the seat of the MacNeils of Barra, an ancestral home since the 15th century. The family were not bashful rulers. Each day a herald would sound a horn from the castle, before declaring: 'Hear oh ye people, and listen oh ye nations: The great MacNeil of Barra having finished his meal, the princes of the earth may now dine.' Razed in the 18th century, the MacNeils sold Kisimul in 1837. Robert Lister MacNeil, an American architect who succeeded to the title of clan chief in 1914, made it his life's purpose to restore the ruin, eventually purchasing Kisimul, as well as a large chunk of land on Barra, in 1937. Repairs to the castle began the following year, with walls being re-erected and internal buildings made habitable.

There seemed to be two ways to reach Kisimul: by motor boat or by swimming. I chose the simpler option, joining three others, a middle-aged American tourist, wearing sunglasses despite the drizzle, and two Scottish exiles, for the two-minute ferry crossing. I followed the American out of the boat and up steps to the castle.

'It's so small. I thought it would be bigger,' she pronounced in a southern American drawl.

Indeed, the castle was small, measuring just 40 metres across at its widest point. The size enhanced its charm. I guess when one hails from Arizona – a state the size of Britain and Ireland together, and boasting the Grand Canyon – everything seems meagre in comparison.

The builders were in. Workmen mooched about the

courtyard, banging and drilling. A wooden walkway was being installed beneath the battlements. I meandered through the castle: along the gravel paths of the little courtyard, into the mortuary chapel, where Robert Lister MacNeil is buried, up the stairs of the white-walled hall, past rows of mounted brown besses, taken from the field of Culloden in 1746. A picture on one of the walls was of Kisimul in 1906; it was a dilapidated, falling down structure, unrecognisable from the castle of today. I climbed the stone steps to the tower house, believed to be the oldest part of the castle, and looked towards Castlebay, imagining I was the herald barking commands to MacNeil's subjects on Barra.

I ran up Heaval. Or – if this is to be a true account – I climbed Heaval in the guise of a runner: wearing shorts and a T-shirt, running shoes on my feet. First on road, then on ever-steepening grass slopes, the ascent was unexpectedly arduous. The gradient had not looked so abrupt when viewed from Kisimul. Running gradually gave way to a resigned walk. Day-trippers began to pass me. Two-thirds of the way to the summit, as I passed a white marble statue depicting the Madonna holding a child aloft on her left shoulder, I began to question my sanity. Why I was doing this, why I was putting myself through such misery? Partly I wanted to emulate the runners who take part in an annual race up and down Heaval. Competitors start in Castlebay, climb to the highest point, before tearing downhill to the finish line in the village. The record is a sickening 26 minutes. I did not time myself, but the record was not under threat.

The summit was in sight. I forced myself to run, breaking into a shuffle, dragging stubborn limbs upwards. My legs felt as if they had run the Goatfell and Isles of Jura races back to back. But then a joyful moment: there was no more up. I raised my eyes to a wondrous vision below: Castle Bay and Vatersay, with a procession of green islands, fringed with white, beyond. It almost made the toil worthwhile. A couple were standing by the summit trig pillar. They were sporty types, sharp-featured and tanned, wearing proper walking boots and branded outdoor clothes. We exchanged cameras. The woman took a photograph of me, the magnificence of the southern islands in the background. I then took a photograph of them, smiling and embracing. I felt a prick of jealousy at their intimacy.

The formalities over, the man asked if I was competing in the annual Barrathon, the island's creatively-named half-marathon race, or the Hebridean Challenge, a multi-island race of cycling, hill-running, sea-kayaking and swimming, both taking place that month. I was doing neither, I shrugged. He was doing the Barrathon, he told me. He had done the Hebridean Challenge before, but not this year.

There begin a rally of machismo: man versus man, a battle to be the alpha male of Heaval. He served his half-marathon personal best at me. I returned mine – a better one – to his forehand. He retaliated with an account of an epic Cairngorms race he had recently taken part in. I pushed him to the base line by slicing back the Highland Cross. His girlfriend rolled her eyes. And so it went on. I emerged as the clear winner, by my reckoning. After all, I had run up Heaval (he was not to know I had walked most of the way), and he had definitely walked all the way.

It was cold on the summit, so cold the wind brought tears to my eyes. I wanted to return to Castlebay, to kick off my shoes, to lie down and sleep. The couple were watching though, expectant. I was a hardened hill runner, the alpha male of this hill. Conquering Heaval was just the beginning. I had to prove my mettle. I waved a resigned goodbye and set off to the north, running in the direction of one of Heaval's minor tops. The going was straightforward and mercifully downhill. That was until I reached a boggy col, where the land began to rise again. I cursed every miserable step. Reaching the top, I glanced back at the summit of Heaval. The couple were gone. Enough was enough. I retraced my steps to Heaval and fled downhill to Castlebay.

I took a bus to the north of Barra, travelling along winding roads in ponderous silence with three others, before disembarking at the airport. Here Barra narrows to a width of scarcely 400 metres and is virtually flat, with only a strip of grassland and a mass of sand dunes separating the east and west shores. The terminal was a small, squat building perched on the edge of Tràigh Mhòr, a vast, sweeping bay. To the unknowing, there is a glaring and vital omission from Barra airport: a runway.

When proposals for an airport on Barra were first raised in the early-1930s, islanders looked to their beautiful beaches, prompting John MacPherson, a contemporary of Compton Mackenzie, to suggest Tràigh Mhòr. Here was a natural landing strip: compact, flat, hard and spacious. Scheduled air services to and from Barra, using runways twice-daily washed by the tide, commenced three years later in 1936. Around the same time a passenger terminal also opened on land close to Gatwick racecourse in Sussex. Gatwick would expand to become one of the busiest and largest airports in the world. On Barra, time has stood still. Tràigh Mhòr remains the island's landing strip, the only commercial airport of its kind in the world. At high tide the three runways – marked by poles in the sand – disappear beneath the waves.

A crowd was congregating on the beach-side, anticipating the arrival of the 3.40pm service from Benbecula. The strand was now empty, vacated by the beachcombers and cockle pickers that were a short time earlier flitting across the 'runways'. Signs warn people to keep off the beach when a windsock is flying, indicating the airport is active and a landing imminent. The simple notices seem to suffice: security fences synonymous with air travel are redundant on Barra.

I imagined the Twin Otter plane taking off from Benbecula, steadily gaining height, the crinkled eastern edge of South Uist ever shrinking. Perhaps passengers might be able to glimpse St Kilda to the west? Crossing the sounds of Eriskay and Barra, where ships would be bobbing in the swell, the Twin Otter would begin its descent to the beach-fringed island of Barra. There can be few finer air journeys.

I had been looking east, expecting the plane to sweep over Fuday and another Orosay, before approaching Tràigh Mhòr, when a whirr of propeller blades sounded behind me, from the west. An instant later the Twin Otter zipped low over my head, touching down on the beach, a torrent of water thrown up in its wake. The aircraft, still travelling away from the terminal, quickly came to a stop and spun around, before parking neatly in front of the airport building. I felt like applauding. A door swung open and six passengers used steps to disembark. The pilot leaped out of the cockpit. A little tractor carrying a trailer rolled onto the sand to ferry the meagre baggage to the terminal.

Not long after the plane was speeding across the sand of Tràigh Mhòr again, a new batch of passengers onboard, seemingly on a collision course with white houses on a distant shore when it lifted quickly. The Twin Otter rose into the eastern sky, now cloudy and grey. Silence replaced the slice of the propellers. Soon the plane had vanished, destined for a very different runway at Glasgow airport.

The onlookers made for their cars. The arriving passengers were whisked away. The café at the terminal closed. I walked the short distance across the island to the west coast, arriving at Tràigh Eais, a deserted mile-and-a-half stretch of beach. I stared out across the ocean, contemplating the awesome distance to North America. This really did seem like the end of the world. The western sky was blackening. Trouble was brewing over the Atlantic – and it was heading to Barra. I sat down to eat on the beach, but was driven away by the pestering of sand flies.

I trudged eastwards along the road that clings to the curve of Tràigh Mhòr, continuing along a route signposted to a ferry terminal at Àird Mhòr, the departure point for Eriskay. The weather had worsened: the dark, heavy clouds were now overhead, the wind whipped at the hood of my waterproof. Drizzle emerged from those clouds, soaking the land. Beautiful Barra was beginning to look ugly. I continued along the lonely road, feet aching, blisters forming on heels. My mood was black. I cursed the man who had warned me of this weather, the forecaster who had been proved right.

And then, a glimmer of hope: I could escape Barra. I had intended to spend two nights on the island, but why not leave tonight? I was destined for the terminal, anyway. Perhaps I could make the last crossing to Eriskay? I could not recall the afternoon ferry times, but surely there would be one more crossing today? My thoughts flashed forward. Once on Eriskay, I could travel north and stay in a hostel on South Uist, negating the need to camp on what looked likely to be a filthy night.

Foolish hopes. I was too late. The last ferry had sailed. I should have realised sooner. I had not seen a car for half an hour. The road would have been busy with ferry traffic going to and from the terminal had a sailing been looming. The empty car park at the windswept terminal confirmed the fact.

I was to spend one more night on Barra. I checked the ferry timetable. The next sailing was at 7am. I weighed up my alternatives. There were really only two. I could return to the junction and attempt to catch a bus to Castlebay, where I could sleep undercover, then return to Àird Mhòr in the morning. Or I could sit it out here, find a sheltered spot to camp and hope the weather was not too cruel.

I chose the second option. At least then I could catch the first ferry in the morning. The obvious problem was finding a sanctuary from the wind. I had no time to procrastinate; rain was falling horizontally and wind blowing frantically. I followed the line of a barbed wire fence, which ran along the edge of the car park and continued towards the sea. I hurled over my belongings, then threw myself over. From a little knoll on the other side of the fence, I looked down to the shore, a frothy sea beyond. There was a flat, grassy oblong of ground, seemingly sheltered by the arm of a slipway. It would have to do. I hurriedly erected the tent and surrounded it with a ring of securing rocks, before retreating inside. It was 6pm, 13 hours until the next ferry. A long, friendless night beckoned.

An hour passed. The rain was easing but the wind was growing. I slithered from my sleeping bag to put in place another circle of boulders. The situation looked even more desperate from the outside. The tent rocked alarmingly, swaying to and fro, utterly at the whim of the wind. I pitied then ridiculed myself. Why had I chosen this wretched campsite over a safe, warm bed in Castlebay or South Uist?

Dusk arrived early. I had been dozing lightly when I woke with a start to find the buffeting had increased. The wind had changed direction. The gusts were now coming directly off the sea. The slipway no longer gave me any protection. I grew fearful. The canvas cracked and whistled like a whip. I added yet more stones, including a low wall between the tent and the sea. It was a pointless venture but it made the minutes disappear with greater haste. I crouched close to the ground as I carted the rocks to the tent, fearing a freak gust could lift me off my feet.

As I constructed the wall, a black outline bobbing on the sea caught my eye: a seal. The creature stared back at me, oblivious to the furore around it. The seal disappeared beneath the swell, re-emerging some twenty metres away. He turned his gaze on me again. Another seal surfaced close by, with the creature also fixing his eyes on mine. Like synchronised swimmers, they dived together, and I would not see them again.

Back in the tent, the noise was tremendous: a ceaseless battering, a low moaning. My thoughts ran wild. I remembered the story of a camper on a Glencoe campsite being hurled into a tree, breaking his leg, when a gust ripped his tent from the ground. I had visions of being tossed into the sea, dashing my head against the rocks, trapped in the inner sheet, frantically struggling to escape, only to succumb to the cold, choppy water, drowning horribly. In these grim, uncertain minutes came a moment of light relief: the thought of Private James Frazer, the *Dad's Army* gloom merchant whose home was Barra, uttering his immortal catchphrase: 'We're doomed.'

It was 2am. The wind was ferocious, lashing my little tent. I was helpless and filled with dread. Rain drilled thunderously on the canvas. I unzipped the inner sheet and laid my hand on the roof of the tent, clasping my fingers around the shuddering pole. I sensed that the dreadful moment: my home being seized from the earth, lifted up, thrown and torn, was near. I braced myself. The minutes passed slowly. I concentrated on the wind, attempting to read its sighs and moans. The noise became voices, awful, ethereal cries from high above. The blasts of air arrived in rolling waves, roaring closer, louder, stronger, then breaking over the tent, shaking its foundations, petrifying its occupant. The power of nature seemed boundless. Sooner or later a rogue wave would come, one bigger than all the rest, the greatest, the most powerful, the one that would lift me into the sea.

I could bear it no longer.

I have to move. I have to get out of here.

I flung my belongings into a now sodden rucksack and wrenched on waterproofs. Emerging unto the wrath, I commenced the delicate task of dismantling the tent. First I removed the circle of stones, flinging them into the sea, apart from two large boulders which I used to weigh down the canvas to prevent the wind stealing it. Then I flattened the tent, whipped out the poles and bundled the sheets into a bag. I headed uphill, away from the thrashing sea, crossed the fence and raced across the car park to the shelter of the terminal building. I tried the two doors. One was the entrance to the café and a waiting area. The second, on the opposite side of the building, was solid and wooden, concealing what lay on the other side. Both were locked.

I waited for dawn, willing the dark hours to subside. I sat on a hard floor, sheltering in the lee of the building, growing increasingly cold. But I was glad to have escaped the tent. It would have been blown away by now. The storm had grown worse. Daybreak came, grey and subdued. Yet lightness revealed a ray of hope: a key, lost or deliberately left in a crevice by the terminal building. I tried the wooden door first. The lock fell open. Startled but elated, I stumbled inside. The room was rectangular and windowless, with wooden shelves lining the walls and rope coiled on the ground. It was better than the best hotel; it was merciful shelter. I lay prostrate on the floorboards, looking up to the ceiling, musing on my upturned fortunes.

I vacated the storeroom before the ferrymen arrived, not wanting them to think I had broken in. I locked the door and returned the key to the place I had found it. The ferry, which was tied up on the pier, was due to leave Àird Mhòr at 7am. I reckoned the crew would turn up at 6am. But it was half an hour after that time before headlights appeared through the gloom. The driver sped past me and parked on the pier. A man dressed in yellow waterproofs gingerly emerged from the vehicle, before moving rapidly down to the ship before I could call out. Another member of the crew, clad in the same attire, arrived shortly after, then two more. Not much longer, I reassured myself. I stood in the doorway of the café, scanning the boat for signs of action, listening for the sound of an engine starting up. But nothing was happening. The sea was angry and frothing. The weather was not worse, but not better. A pall of mist hung over Barra, seemingly immovable and permanent.

And then it dawned on me. This ship is going nowhere.

The departure time came and went. One of the crew materialised from the ship and ran up the pier to tell me what I had guessed, what I did not want to believe. I was crushed. I asked when the waiting room would be unlocked, when the café would open, if it would ever open. He was vague. An hour, maybe two, he was not sure.

I waited. No-one came. An hour slipped past, tortuously slow. These were the worst moments, my lowest ebb. I huddled in the doorway, impatient and shivering. I was contemplating a return to the store room when I heard the splash of tyres on the car park and a door slamming. It was the cleaner. I wanted to embrace her, to thank her, to tell how long I had craved her arrival. She stood at the door, fumbling with a set of keys. I lingered behind like a slathering dog, fighting the urge to snatch the keys off her and open the door myself.

She sloshed a mop across the floor and left. As the door slammed shut, I turned on the radiators and stripped to my underwear, laying wet clothes and shoes on the heat to dry. The room was soon filled with a musty scent of mud and sweat. I leaned back on one of the benches, gazing out of the window at the commotion of rain and wind outside, soon drifting into sleep. I woke abruptly to the sound of foreign voices. I had been asleep for no longer than five minutes. Two people, a young French couple, stood before me, the woman repeatedly uttering 'pardon, pardon' and not knowing where to look or whether to turn and run. I grabbed half-dry, steaming clothes from the radiator, apologised profusely for the smell and hurried into a toilet cubicle to make myself decent.

The wind was easing and the rain had abated. A second ferry due to depart at 9am had been cancelled, but a third – the 11am sailing – was expected to happen. The waiting room was full and expectant, anticipation of an announcement growing. The place now smelt of bacon and coffee. I had no change, but a waiting passenger sympathised with my plight and thrust a mug of tea into my hand. The simplicity of the gesture made me glad, and I thanked him profusely. Occasionally my eyes met those of the French mademoiselle, who returned a stare of bemusement. Good news filtered through: the furore had subsided enough for a crossing of the Sound of Barra to be attempted. I cheered inwardly, hurrying down the pier to board the vessel before the captain could change his mind. As the ship pulled clear of the pier and manoeuvred around the slipway, I glanced at my campsite, recalling the misery of the night. I did not look back again. Never had I been so relieved to leave an island as Barra.

15

Berneray

On the beach, you can live in bliss.
Dennis Wilson

✧

What is the difference between a Scottish beach and a Thai beach? Not a great deal, it seems.

A British expat living in Thailand was visiting a tourist centre on Koh Chang when a photograph, purportedly of the island's Kai Bae beach, engaged his attention. To the casual observer, nothing was amiss. Here was an illustration of the beauty of the Koh Chang coastline: white-sand beaches, a cobalt sea, swaying palm trees. It was unquestionably a Thai paradise.

Or not, for something was indeed amiss. This was no Thai beach; it was a Berneray beach, located on a different continent, some 6000 miles away. The hills in the far distance were the clincher. These were not Thai hills; they were Harris hills.

The expat, Ian McNamara, who runs a guesthouse on Koh Chang, revealed the story to the world – and the world was amused.

'Pedantic nit-pickers may point out that there aren't actually any mountain ranges visible from Kai Bae beach,' McNamara said. 'But is still a nice photo. And so what if the beach in the photo is really located on the isle of Berneray in Scotland? I loved the photo of the pure white sand and those rolling hills in the distance.' He went on: 'That's a bit odd, because last time I looked there weren't any offshore mountain ranges visible from Kai Bae beach – only sea.'

The picture, it emerged, had been taken four years earlier by photographer John Kirriemuir, and was subsequently posted on a website marketing Berneray. He had forgotten of its existence – until Thai tourism chiefs claimed the beach as their own. Rather than sourcing an image of Kai Bae, officials deemed an Outer Hebridean offering to be a suitable stand-in. The strand in question is the simply-named West Beach, an astoundingly beautiful strip of pale sand that runs along the entire western periphery of Berneray. It was a worthy stand-in.

Updating his blog, Kirriemuir wrote: 'True, there are some similarities; great sand, unpolluted sea. But also some differences; if you swim off both beaches, you would very quickly realise what one of them is.'

The sea off Berneray is indeed a little on the frigid side, not quite Arctic, but certainly nippier than the balmy waters of the Gulf of Thailand.

But that was not the point. This was: not only could Kai Bae and West Beach be innocently confused (the oversight had not been noticed until McNamara's intervention), but that the confusion was perfectly feasible. A Berneray beach would not look out of place on Koh Chang, and a Koh Chang beach would not look out of place on Berneray. The islands should consider a twinning arrangement.

The episode was a public relations triumph for Berneray, the best piece of marketing Visit Scotland never did. A spokesman for the organisation later said: 'They do say imitation is the most sincere form of flattery, so although the use of the photo of a beach on the Isle of Berneray to represent a Thai beach is somewhat misleading, I'm sure it is a compliment in disguise.'

*

When the temperature falls to 18C on Koh Chang, it is considered chilly, time to pull on long johns – or whatever may be the Thai equivalent. If the mercury reaches 18C on the Hebrides, islanders are in heat wave territory. The climatic conditions of the Long Island can be grim; that is no secret. Rain will fall for days, high winds will blow unabated. The gusts buffeting the other Berneray, the island at the southern tip of the Western Isles, are so fierce that fish are plucked from the sea and deposited on the tops of the 190-metre cliffs of Skate Point.

Geoff Spice, a retired merchant banker who spent a month living as a castaway on the treeless Sound of Harris island of Sgarabhaigh in 2009, as he attempted to beat a 40-a-day smoking habit, had to be evacuated as the tail end of Hurricane Bill blasted the Western Isles. 'The weather made me a prisoner of my tent,' Spice declared. 'Sometimes it was diabolical. It was bloody awful. The wind was unbelievable.' The month was August.

The ultimate cost of the weather in the west is human life. When a severe storm struck the islands in 2005, with 110mph winds accompanying a tidal surge, a family-of-five perished as they attempted to flee their flood-threatened home on South Uist.

Weather, chiefly its unpredictability, is the reason the islands will never be corrupted by mass tourism. Even if the weather is fine (and it can be, for days on end), Scotland has another natural check on tourism – the midge. Despite its relative smallness, Britain – which would fit into Russia 78 times – has an extraordinary range of micro-climates. The maximum average temperature in Stornoway is 11C; in London it is 14C. Rain falls on Stornoway 201 days a year; in London it precipitates on 106. Yet the watery surroundings mean the weather is subject to abrupt change – for better and for worse. Today's weather was undergoing an expeditious transformation, mercifully, for the better.

The sea in the Sound of Barra was a shifting, sloshing, swirling cauldron. Starting the journey to Eriskay below deck, I lounged in the warmth, contented to watch the ferry battle the fierce currents of the channel from behind a window. Then a seasick child, green-faced, vomited profusely into a bin at my side; I swiftly abandoned my position, climbing a flight of metal steps to the deck. This is where I should have been from the beginning. The sea was furious, its power boundless. The ferry sunk into troughs and soared onto peaks, leaving an empty feeling in stomachs, like being in a car crossing a humped-back bridge at speed. Showers of icy sea water, flung upwards, rained onto the deck. I could taste salt on my lips. The air seemed the purest I had ever breathed.

A series of buses conveyed me north. A Royal Mail post bus, stopping at every post box, rattled along the rolling roads of Eriskay and across the causeway to South Uist, depositing me in Daliburgh. The conversation never deviated from the weather, from the previous night's great storm. The tent of a group of boys camping on North Uist was ripped to pieces, said one passenger. The gusts were so strong on Berneray – my ultimate destination – that stones from a nearby beach were flung against cars, another said.

The post lady was rather more direct. 'You call that a storm? You should come here in winter.'

The day was brightening. The western sky was blue. The once mist-capped hills of South Uist were clear. A miserable morning was becoming a magical afternoon. The sunshine gained in intensity, becoming brilliant and blinding. It seemed unthinkable that nature had been in such a recent rage. A second bus lumbered north, passing through South Uist, Benbecula, Grimsay and North Uist, the outlook an ever-changing panorama of machair and peat, loch and sea. I could not eavesdrop on conversations because the speakers were Gaelic. Benbecula and South Uist remain the stronghold of Gaelic-speaking in Scotland. Unlike in the Highlands, Gaelic names on road signs came first, written in larger print than the English translations below.

A final bus went as far as Baile, the service's Berneray terminus, close to MacLeod's 'gunnery', the oldest building on the island. The house was the birthplace of Sir Norman MacLeod, a determined royalist who fought against the Roundheads led by Oliver Cromwell at the battle of Worcester in 1651. MacLeod was captured and imprisoned in the Tower of London, but he escaped to Europe. Following the restoration of the monarchy in 1660, Macleod was knighted by Charles II. Free to return to Berneray, MacLeod turned his birthplace into an armoury and built a new home for himself nearby.

Beyond the gunnery stood a pair of converted black-houses serving as a youth hostel. The hostel was one of four in the Western Isles run by the Gatliff Trust, a charitable organisation enabling islanders to run traditional crofts as basic hostels. The others were on Harris, Lewis and South Uist, but the quartet share a common feature: they are located amid scenes of remoteness and natural exquisiteness. The thatched-roofed hostel on Berneray is arguably the finest of the four, standing so close to the shore it seems certain the sea will one day claim the building for itself. Beds were allocated on a first-come, first-served basis. All were taken when I arrived, so I pitched my tent behind a ruined cottage within the hostel grounds.

I crossed the interior of Berneray to reach West Beach, first walking along the shoreline of East Beach – another wondrous but plainly-named strip – and then ascending grassy slopes to the highest point on the island. The summit of Beinn Shléibhe is a marvellous vantage point from which to survey the islands dotted about the Sound of Harris, yet it does not do West Beach justice. From here, the beach appears as a narrow, undistinguished sliver of sand, merely demarcating green meadows and blue sea. More impressive was the vision of the isle of Pabbay, a barren, rugged place, two miles off Berneray's north-western seaboard, where almost 350 people once lived before the population was removed in the 1840s.

I descended to West Beach, recalling the words of Hamish Haswell-Smith, who in his comprehensive book on the Scottish islands, gushingly described the strand as 'one of the loveliest stretches of white shell-sand beach in Britain – about four kilometres of perfection'. And Haswell-Smith was writing before the beach became embroiled in a marketing campaign for a Thai resort. Even so – perfection? With that weighty billing, West Beach could only disappoint, I reckoned.

As I reached the lower slopes of Beinn Shléibhe, West Beach revealed itself: a vision of calm and tranquillity, a vision of unerring beauty. I paused on the edge of the machair for some moments, then – removing my shoes – I walked onto the beach with careful, deliberate strides, as if the sand between my toes was hallowed. I looked left and right, scouring the place for people, overwhelmed with a sense that I was trespassing on the perfection described by Haswell-Smith. The beach was deserted. There were not even footprints in the sand. I looked for fault, tried to find imperfection. I found none. Offshore, empty islands sprung from turquoise waters. To the north rose Harris, its highest mountains peeping through the gap between the impressive hilltop of Ceapabhal, itself almost an island, and the village of Northton.

I meandered in the direction of the rocks of Rubha

Bhoisinnis, unhurried, unflustered. Gulls and oyster catchers called to one another overhead. I stopped to skim flat pebbles, counting their bounces on the water. I hurled round or misshapen rocks, the ones unsuitable for skimming, as far as I could into the ocean. I watched the flight of the missile, listened for a reassuring plop, then imagined the stone dropping slowly, coming to rest in its new submerged home. I scooped warm sand into my hands, allowing the grains to slip gently over my palms. I poked my sandy fingers into marooned pools of seawater, collected in rocks that ran in occasional ribbons across the beach, hoping to see the flicker of a fish or the sideways motion of a clumsy crustacean. I built a sandcastle, a grand Scottish fortification. I dug out a moat and patted the sides. I wished I had a flag, a Saltire, to raise on the battlements. I would have liked to have waited for the sea to come in, surrounding the castle, breaking it up, gradually flattening it, until its existence was nullified. I did not want to wait, so I ran at the castle, kicking the sand, kicking my creation to smithereens.

I paddled in the cold water, immersing my legs up to my knees, before returning to the shore. I splashed water over my face, drenched my hair and slicked it back. I waded back out into the blue, this time staying longer, venturing deeper, my body gradually hardening to the coldness. I roamed haphazardly along the beach again, scarcely knowing if I was walking north or south. A shell would catch my attention, either its colour or shape. I would hold it up, turn it round, clean it of sand, inspect it. Most I discarded; the rest I dropped into a pocket. The sun continued to blaze from a cloudless sky. Still there was no-one to disturb me. The day seemed as if it could last forever; I yearned it would. I had discovered paradise, the most exquisite Hebridean island of them all: Berneray, my desert island.

When Visit Scotland surveyed UK residents asking them

to identify a picture of Berneray, just twenty-two per cent of respondents correctly guessed the image was a Scottish scene. Others wrongly assumed the photograph must have been taken in Mauritius, New Zealand or Thailand. Berneray, today, could have been the double, the spitting image, of any one of those far-flung, romantic destinations.

But why should Berneray simply be comparable? In Scotland, on the Outer Hebrides, on Berneray, on West Beach: this was incomparable, unsurpassable.

As I swung open the door of the hostel kitchen, eight faces turned to look at me. They were sailors, although, by their own admittance, not terribly successful ones. They were more likely to potter about the Hebrides than sail across the Atlantic. Travelling together for 23 years, they were bonded by a common love of Scotland's west coast islands. Which was just as well as they were marooned on Berneray, waiting for the wind to change direction before they could relocate to a new Hebridean island.

One of the men handed me a bowl of mussels, collected from East Beach several hours earlier. Another laid a tumbler before me and poured a glass of whisky, the measure approaching a triple. They insisted I join their table.

Dinner was to be followed by a party, a Berneray-style party. Two 20-something women hostellers, nurses from Glasgow, joined the jamboree. Ukuleles were brought out. Song sheets were distributed. Kazoos, tambourines, castanets and whistles were allocated. Those without instruments were issued with saucepans and wooden spoons. A debate ensued about the correct way to play the castanets. A nurse demonstrated against her thigh, her one-woman show accompanied by whoops and wolf whistles. A washboard, another instrument, apparently, was unaccounted for. The sailors warmed up their voices, singing comical scales. Glasses were recharged with whisky and wine. And so the singing began: *Lili Marlene, The Bonnie Banks o' Loch Lomond, Whisky in the Jar, Jambalaya, Cockles and Mussels, The Eton Boating Song, Cotton Fields, The Bar with no Beer, Messing About on the River*.

Then the most raucous of them all: *Wild Rover*. Heads bobbed, feet stomped, singing became shouting. The first line of the chorus came: 'And it's no, nay, never . . .' Fists slammed the table – bang, bang, bang – after the 'never', creating waves on the whisky. We had been briefed about an instrumental section. 'Ready?' one of the ukulele players bellowed over the din. 'Now.' Pots and pans were clouted, kazoos tooted, whistles whistled, tambourines shaken and thwacked, castanets clicked. The effect was a hilarious, joyous, thunderous, ridiculous, cacophony of noise.

A German boyfriend and girlfriend had slipped into the room during *Wild Rover*, quietly and almost unseen. The man knew the tune, he said, although the German lyrics bore no resemblance to those of *Wild Rover*. Still, the song was played again, with the version this time sung by two voices in German and far more conservatively. Three others then entered – two Glaswegian men and a diminutive but assured Australian student: a drinking dream team. The trio had been on West Beach, watching the sunset, guzzling red wine and rum. The bottle of whisky did another lap of the table, with the party now 16-strong.

One of the Glaswegians was drunk, slurring slightly. He was handed a song sheet. 'I can't read your English words,' he declared, stressing the word 'your', grinning at the faces of the Englishmen around the table. His fellow newcomer and the Australian shared a seat, exchanging flirty glances and touches.

The fresh recruits added to the volume, rather than the

melody. The songs resumed, many of them corruptions of originals, making reference to the sailors' favourite islands, memorable journeys or each other. We were partway through a tune when the intoxicated Glaswegian abruptly stood up and declared his intention to marry one of the nurses. That is if one counts someone shouting 'will ye marry me?' across a packed room as a marriage proposal. The nurse's cheeks reddened as all eyes focused on her.

'Say 'yes',' a sailor taunted.

She shook her head in astonishment, spitting the word 'no' in the jilted Glaswegian's direction.

I met the trio two nights later on Lewis and asked what had caused the outburst. Before the most-inebriated of the group could offer a defence, the other man blurted out: 'She must have mentioned something about beer, Chinese food or Rangers.'

Midnight had long passed. I had not slept for two days, but I could not leave the party. We sang a Hebrides version of Henry Belafonte's *Islands in the Sun*.

'Islands in the sun, Hebrides you are the ones . . .'

The words would stick in my head for days after.

The sailors then shushed the rest of us as they sang a gentle rendition of *The Mingulay Boat Song*, a tribute to one of their favourite islands.

It is easy to be sentimental over Scotland. I have watched grown men cry as they hear the words of *Caledonia*. We had overdosed on sentiment and were approaching the I-love-you stage of drunkenness when the surroundings are a wonderful place full of wonderful people who are all your friends. It is typically the stage before vomiting.

'That beach,' the Australian said, referring to West Beach, 'is the most beautiful I have ever seen, better than Bondi Beach.'

'Of course it is,' one of the sailors snorted, waving his

hand dismissively, 'this is the most beautiful place in the world.'

The last song, number 30 in the bundle, was sung. The ukuleles were laid down. The dregs in our glasses were drained.

'One more?' the rum-fuelled Glaswegian implored. '*Flower of Scotland.*' We all rose to our feet – an Australian, Germans, Scottish, and, in the greatest numbers of all, English – to answer his request.

He sang the lines about Proud Edward's army returning to England 'tae think again' a mite too forcefully, eyes bulging. Still, it was a fitting climax, like a flag-waving rendition of *Land of Hope and Glory* at the culmination of the Last Night of the Proms. Something stirred deep within my soul, an incredible sadness yet a blissful ecstasy. I was drunk on whisky and Scottish islands. I felt the little hairs on the back of my neck rise in unison, a lump in my throat. And I am sure I saw a tear roll down the cheek of a sailor.

Islands in the sun, Hebrides you are the ones . . .

The lyrics wandered among my thoughts as I walked away from Baile, along Berneray's coast-embracing road. Reaching Borgh, I cut inland, following a route that rose in a shallow valley between two hills, reaching a community hall. Here a track continued over level farmland and machair, ending at the remains of the long-gone settlement of Sheabie. Only the outline of the cottages, marked by low stone walls, overgrown with turf, acted as reminders of the people who once lived here. A one-time island in the Sound of Berneray, Sheabie became attached to the mainland after a sandstorm buried the township, filling the strait between it and the mainland. Repaired buildings were again wrecked in another storm in 1760, before Sheabie was cleared in 1853.

Sheabie overlooked a landmark I had been seeking, the reason I had ventured to the remote, southern extremity of this island: a cairn dedicated to one of Berneray's most famous sons. Standing close to the shoreline, the stone monument marks the location of the home of Angus Mac-Askill, Berneray's tallest man, a real-life giant. Born in 1825 and one of 13 children, Angus grew to a height three inches shy of eight feet and weighed more than 30 stone. He was two feet taller than his father, the palms of his hands were 12 inches long and eight inches wide, and his feet measured 17 inches from heel to toe. After the MacAskill family emigrated to Nova Scotia in 1831, Angus toured North America with a travelling circus, his prodigious height contrasting with General Tom Thumb, a dwarf standing little more than three feet tall. Predictably, Angus became known as Gille Mòr – big boy – or the Cape Breton Giant. Despite having no degenerative defect, Angus died at Cape Breton aged 38. In 1981, the *Guinness Book of Records* described him as the tallest 'true giant' that had ever lived. A plaque on the cairn – as high as Angus was tall – records his life without bluster: 'He achieved many feats of strength and is remembered as a kindly and just man, and a humble Christian.'

The quiet roads of the Western Isles are lauded by cyclists. Pedalling from Barra or South Uist to the Butt of Lewis, the northern rim of the mainland Outer Hebrides, is a compressed version of travelling between Land's End to John o' Groats, and arguably a finer excursion. Sprinters and the super-fit will cover the 150-mile ride in two days. The rest will take three, four and even five days. Only the foolhardy choose to tackle the journey from north to south, for when the prevailing wind is blowing hard even pedalling downhill is an almighty effort.

There were four pairs of cyclists waiting for a ferry to Harris at the Berneray terminal. Two of their number had loftier ambitions than cycling the length of the Western Isles; Peter and Petra were world cyclists. Peter had been cycling non-stop for five years. He had set off from the Netherlands with the intention of reaching Australia within a year. Once he attained his destination, he did not want to stop. He chose a life on the road. What was meant to be a one-year adventure, he said, will last forever. And with a mane-like beard and bright, sharp eyes, the Dutchman had the look of how a round-the-world cyclist should appear.

But Peter's mission is not to cycle around the world, but to cycle through the world, visiting as many countries as possible. In the five years since he left the Netherlands, his country count is in excess of 50, his mileage greater than 40,000. Petra, his Austrian girlfriend, had joined him only for the latest stretch of Peter's odyssey, from Dover to Scotland, before returning – or so the plan was – to the Netherlands via Ireland and England. Like Peter, Petra had pledged to become a full-time travelling cyclist, much to the chagrin of her parents.

I could see the pleasures of their life: an existence dedicated to discovery, to wandering; experiencing new cultures and horizons; the ability to shape your own destiny, not to have it shaped by others. But I could see the pitfalls: the long days of perpetual motion; the absence of creature comforts; living on the breadline; the boredom, the cold, the heat, the hunger; a million other desires and emotions.

'The freedom,' Peter answered when I asked him why he did what he did. 'Not just the freedom of going where you want, but freedom of thought. And not being influenced by society.'

Peter, in his early 30s, and Petra, in her late 20s, tall, tanned and good looking, were no drop-outs. Society had

180

not rejected them; they had rejected society. They were highly educated and qualified; golden futures and fat salaries beckoned. Instead they survive on £1000 a year, take odd jobs to earn that money, camp for free on wild land, rely on the friendship and sofas of strangers, avoid air travel if at all possible and forage for food. In North Uist they had dined on kelp (which tasted like peanuts, Petra said) and limpets.

'I was successful,' Peter said, 'but I felt bad, really unhappy.' So he left. To him, the cycle ride, the journey, is an experience, not a challenge. He did not see the sense in chasing records. 'Look at Mark Beaumont. After cycling around the world, he has now cycled across North and South America, climbing Mount McKinlay and Aconcagua on the way. Why? If you see a bike ride as a race or record, you take on the mentality of what I left behind. You are just doing a different thing with the same mentality.'

And what does a man who has cycled in Columbia, Iran, Pakistan, Patagonia and Tibet make of the Hebrides?

'We've been to Skye, South Uist, Benbecula, North Uist and now here – I find them really beautiful. The clarity of light reminds me of northern parts of Scandinavia. But it's so cold. I prefer warm climates. It's so cold,' he repeated, blowing into his cupped hands.

16

Lewis

Island of heather, island of heather,
island of heather of the high mountains,
where I was reared while young,
my dear Island of Lewis.

William Mackenzie

'Cyclonic.' The word jumped off the page, the last thing I
wanted to read on a weather forecast for the days leading
up to my intended visit to St Kilda. But there it was in black
and white: 'cyclonic.' The outlook for The Minch, the sea
between the Inner and Outer Hebrides was bleak: a force
seven severe gale rising to force nine. Presumably the
conditions in the open water of the Atlantic would be even
worse than The Minch.

It was not a day to be outdoors. I had been due to visit the
Shiant Islands, a group of islands between Harris and Skye
celebrated for their large population of black rats. The trip
was cancelled, obviously. The weather was just too unpre-
dictable. As if to prove its fickle nature, I was half-way to a
supermarket in Tarbert when the heavens opened, with a
torrential rain of biblical proportions falling from a black
sky. Ten minutes later the sun was out.

When the weather was poor on childhood family holidays in Devon or Cornwall, we abandoned the beach in
favour of a 'town day'. Waterproofs at the ready, we would
head to Dartmouth, Kingsbridge or Penzance, and mooch

aimlessly around the shops. It was not that I disliked those days. Only I would rather have been playing on a beach. Today was a 'town day'. It was too windy to hire a bike, too misty to walk in the hills, the sea too choppy to even cross the short stretch of water to Taransay. Yet the 'islands' of Harris and Lewis do not abound with towns. There was really just one option: Stornoway, the administrative head-quarters of the Western Isles and by far the most populous place in the Outer Hebrides.

North I went, over the hills, exiting Harris, entering Lewis.

Stornoway had a long-held romantic appeal in my consciousness. A board game, The Great Game of Britain, was the cause of my affection. Players had to move counters around a railway map of Britain (and Ireland, despite the title of the game). The distinctive outline of Harris and Lewis featured in the top left corner of the map, but the makers of the game neglected to add any other Scottish islands, not even Orkney or Shetland, as if the jagged coastlines would have posed too great a challenge to draw. Stornoway was the most distant destination, despite the town – like the rest of the Western Isles – possessing no railway network. To get there, one had to catch a ferry from Kyle of Lochalsh. It was a place no-one wanted to visit, for it typically resulted in losing the game, unless the rest of your destinations happened to be clustered together. To a boy growing up in the middle of England, Stornoway was distant and remote, as far away as Australia. I never conceived I would one day visit.

Yet here I was, standing at the town's bus station, the smell of a salty sea wafting up my nostrils, wondering what to do. There is little glamour about Stornoway. It is a functional place, dominated by the ferry terminal. For the visitor it is somewhere to re-fuel, to shop, to stock up, before moving on to prettier environs. I felt like a child again, sauntering down Port Street, where the wind funnelled between shops and seagulls squabbled over the sticky remains of fish and chips, with no specific aim or purpose, here only because I could not be somewhere else. I should be on the Shiants now, I thought for the hundredth time. The greatest frustration was the weather: it was not *so* awful. I wanted nature to bare her teeth, to throw lightning bolts, to toss hailstones, to unleash hurricanes and tornados, to do her worst. Then I could accept not being able to go to the Shiants. But this – blustery, grey, the occasional shower – made me seethe. Where was the 'cyclonic' weather?

Enduring Stornoway for two-and-a-half hours, I returned to the bus station. A ticket to anywhere but here, I felt like saying to the bus driver, but I settled on Carloway, a sprawling community on the west coast of Lewis.

I stayed at Garenin, another of the Gatliff hostels and another converted blackhouse. The hostel was one of a number of restored blackhouses, although some are actually white, built on sloping ground above the sea inlet of Loch Garenin. The last inhabitants of the Garenin blackhouses – so called because they were built without chimneys, meaning smoke had to escape through the roof – were moved to nearby council properties in 1973. It took 16 years for a trust to be established to preserve the blackhouses, and the village is now a monument to the islanders who called these smoky buildings home.

There was no music tonight, but the line-up of guests was as diverse as it had been on Berneray: a pair of surfers from Bristol, a different German couple, an archaeology student documenting crannogs on Lewis and Harris and a cyclist who had pedalled 92 miles that day to reach Carloway. I left the entourage to run over green cliffs to Dal Mòr beach, where a trio of surfers bobbed on the waves waiting for a big one, before climbing away from the coast and returning to Carloway. The last two miles were run in pouring rain. The sea, the sky and the mist became indivisible. As the wind whimpered and rain rapped the windows of the hostel, I was thankful to be sleeping indoors.

When Cal Mac proposed the introduction of Sunday sailings between Stornoway and Ullapool on the Scottish mainland, the ferry company not only invoked the wrath of the staunchly Christian islanders, it invoked the wrath of God. Nowhere in the UK is Protestantism stronger than on Harris and Lewis. On these islands, the Sabbath is sacrosanct: pubs and shops close, alcohol is not served, tools are laid down, washing is not put on lines, buses do not run (except to church), leisure centres are empty. And while freight and passenger ferries plied a regular trade between Stornoway and Ullapool on Mondays to Saturdays, when it came to Sundays, the waters of The Minch lay undisturbed. It was a tradition: ferries did not, could not, run on the Sabbath.

But Sabbatarianism was under attack. Sunday flights to and from Stornoway airport began in 2002. A ferry linking Berneray and Harris commenced holy day sailings in 2006. Pressure was also mounting on sporting operators to throw open facilities – golf clubs, football pitches and swimming pools – on Sundays. Sabbath sailings were seen as the last bastion of Sabbatarianism, a point of principle worth fighting for. Fight they did; thousands of people opposed Sunday ferries.

Cal Mac dismissed the furious protests. The operator had its own point of principle: by withholding a Sabbath ferry out of respect for the views of traditionalists, the human rights of others to travel on a Sunday were being infringed. The ferry firm was effectively breaking the law. And so it came to pass. On July 17, 2009, the first Sabbath sailing would leave Stornoway, it was announced. Or perhaps not? Two days before the scheduled service, the cross-Minch ferry, the MV *Isle of Lewis*, broke down. Services between Stornoway and Ullapool were cancelled. The ferry could be out of action for 48 hours, Cal Mac warned. Divine intervention? That was how opponents interpreted the timing: it was an act of God.

The Reverend Angus Smith, who lay down on the slipway at Kyleakin in 1965 to protest against the inaugural Sunday ferry to Skye, told the *Scotsman*: 'God is in all providence. The chief message is not that the ferry has broken down, but that God speaks to us through his works. All companies – including ferry companies – should remember to keep the Sabbath holy instead of pursuing monetary gain.'

Other Christians claimed God had the power to sink a Sunday ferry. Strong, headline-grabbing rhetoric, but were the words too strong? The fearful language was doing little to garner public support.

Even if the mechanical breakdown was an act of God, the Almighty could not prevent engineers repairing MV *Isle of Lewis* in time for the Sunday sailing. As she departed Stornoway, with almost 400 passengers on board, Christians who had gathered outside the terminal building uttered psalms. Proponents of Sabbath crossings cheered and clapped. Passengers were in equally good cheer. Musicians returning to the mainland from the Hebridean Celtic Festival on Lewis performed an impromptu ceilidh. MV *Isle of Lewis* arrived in Ullapool, unscathed and unsunk.

But, as the saying goes, God moves in mysterious ways. The first Sabbath sailing from Stornoway was followed the next weekend by a second; there would be no U-turn from Cal Mac. A gay civil partnership ceremony – the first on

Lewis – was staged the next day. Less than 24 hours later, a tornado ripped through Stornoway, dislodging slates, uprooting trees and flipping a car on to its roof. The tornado came ashore at the ferry terminal.

Divine intervention?

It was the Sabbath, so I went to church. There were two Protestant places of worship in Carloway: the Church of Scotland and the Free Church of Scotland. The buildings stand side-by-side at the heart of the village, overlooking Loch Carloway. The faiths of both denominations are based on the same Christian principles, but the Free Church is the more devout, particularly when it comes to the adherence of the Sabbath. One of the moral laws followed by the church is the Fourth Commandment: 'Remember the Sabbath day, to keep it holy.' In that context, the ferry debate is black and white – Sunday sailings leaving Stornoway do not keep the Sabbath holy.

The word 'free' can be confusing, for it hints at liberalism, rather than its true meaning: democracy. Up to the early 19th century, Church of Scotland ministers were chosen by estate owners or wealthy patrons. The practice was opposed by parishes in Auchterarder, Dunkeld and Strathbogie during a 10-year period of confliction. A schism would not happen until 1843 when dozens of ministers and elders walked out of a Church of Scotland general assembly in Edinburgh. Later that day they met Thomas Chalmers at what became known as the Disruption Assembly. Chalmers then founded the Free Church, becoming its first moderator. The tradition of democracy enshrined in 1843 continues today: Free Church ministers and elders are chosen by their congregations.

I was, and still am, and probably always will be, a nonbeliever. I am not a Christian, nor am I an atheist. Agnosticism is a loose term, but my beliefs fall into that broad category. Non-believer or not, Kenny Macleod, the minister of Carloway Free Church, assured me I would be received well in his church. I was nervous, nevertheless, as I walked a long mile from Garenin to Carloway, more nervous than I had been on the start line of the Jura race. I tugged apprehensively at the elastic cord on the hood of my coat. I knew I would be an outsider: not only an Englishman, but an agnostic Englishman.

The car park was jammed. The traffic on the roads was overwhelmingly church-bound. Stepping inside the building, I was greeted with firm handshakes from two elders, who handed me a Bible, psalm book and service sheet. I took a seat in the back row, next to a woman who instantly guessed I was a stranger. Everyone seemed to know everyone else in Lewis, let alone Carloway; I was bound to stand out. There were fifty people scattered about the pews, with another ten arriving in the final minutes before midday. All were smartly dressed: men in suits, women in dresses and hats. These people – adherents of the Free Church – are known as Wee Frees, a colloquialism that has become shorthand for a denomination of deeply-conservative, God-fearing islanders. Just to confuse matters, members of another Christian group, the Free Presbyterian Church of Scotland, are known as Wee Wee Frees.

With the congregation seated, several elders took up seats at the front of the church, along with a precentor who would lead the singing of the psalms. Next Kenny marched down an aisle. Psalms were sung, prayers said. Kenny gave a 40 minute sermon entitled *Do we believe in Jesus?* There were further psalms. The precentor would begin, with the congregation joining in on the second or third word of each verse, singing enthusiastically but not emphatically. It was not joyous, but nor was it joyless. There was no choir and

188

the singing of hymns was prohibited (The Free Church General Assembly voted in November 2010 to allow congregations to use musical instruments and sing hymns). The church walls were undecorated. The mood was serious, reflective.

I considered myself a hypocrite. Why should I be in this church? What right do I have to be here? It was akin to Kenny attending a meeting of atheists. Yet I am in awe of religious buildings: the atmosphere, the architecture, the sense of community and common purpose, the music, even if the songs are in praise of a superior being whose existence I doubt. And I was awed by this congregation, its unshakeable faith, however incredible I found that faith. They made me feel as if my life was empty, lacking somehow.

I was invited to lunch at the manse. Kenny, his wife Maggie and their three children had lived here for five-and-a-half years after he received the call from the congregation in Carloway. He spent six years as an elder at a church in Inverness prior to that calling. Brought up on Scalpay, an island connected to the east coast of Harris by a bridge, Kenny was working as a joiner on the oil yards of the east Highlands when he converted to Christianity. He was 24.

'I just thought that there had to be more to life than this,' he said. 'I felt drawn to God.'

We were joined by DJ, a youth worker and a member of the Church of Scotland. Our pre-lunch conversation inexorably led into a debate about creationism and evolution.

DJ was insistent about his faith. 'I can't believe that anyone believes in evolution and I am flabbergasted that intelligent people believe that man evolved from apes. It's beyond me. In every way human beings are superior and unique.'

'It's creation that makes mankind unique and in God's image,' Kenny chipped in.

I held my tongue, not because I was a guest, but because their belief in creationism was far stronger than my belief in evolution. Kenny knew I was not a Christian. But he did not challenge my principles, so why should I question his? The more I dwelled on the debate, the more I doubted what I actually did believe. I probably knew more about creationism than evolution, yet I blindly followed the latter path. For a multitude of reasons – education, society, upbringing – evolution was lodged in my psyche.

Since arriving on the Western Isles I had listened sceptically to many unsavoury Sabbath tales, some possibly true, some certainly false and some undoubtedly exaggerated. One was an instance of bricks being hurled through windows of a home where washing was drying outside. Another was demands from church elders to cease building work after banging was heard emanating from inside a home. I had also encountered religious hostility from non-Christian islanders and tourists. Such comments boiled down to ignorance, of course, but I found them odd. Lewis is a deeply Christian place where the Sabbath is observed. That should be respected, regardless of opinions to the contrary. Doing anything else is as illogical as a woman visiting a devoutly Muslim country and parading about in a bikini.

I hardly dared to utter such stories in the presence of Kenny and DJ, but I relayed them all the same since there would not be many days when I would have an audience with a Free Church of Scotland minister.

There are no rules governing what people should and should not do on the Sabbath, although going to the cinema, dancing and sport are generally off the agenda, Kenny explained. Nor are congregations told that they must not mow lawns or warned to refrain from exercising or going for a walk. God does not dispense his judgement in such ways, apparently. 'If you are going to win people to come to church,' Kenny said, 'that's the wrong way of going about it.'

Turning to the thorny issue of the Sabbath ferry he said: 'If it comes on a Sunday, then it's going to be like any other day. The Sabbath is a day to enjoy, a day to spend with family. When I worked on the oil yards, I didn't want to be promoted because I knew it would mean working on Sundays. I was asked whether I was 'not allowed'. It's not a rule. It's not about being allowed or not allowed. I believed Sunday should be a day to spend with my family.'

The conversation broke free of religion; Kenny told me about the *Iolaire* disaster.

It was New Year's Day in 1919 and an eager crowd was gathered at the harbour in Stornoway for the arrival of the ship *Iolaire*. Onboard were 284 men, predominately from Lewis, but also from Berneray and Harris, who had survived the battlefields of World War I. The lights of the harbour – representing home – were in sight when the ship struck a reef known as the Beasts of Holm. The ship was wrecked, the lifeboats were swamped, 205 men – weighed down by heavy boots and uniforms – perished. It was tragedy on an unimaginable scale. These young men were survivors of the Great War, yet died yards from shore. They were meant to be the lucky ones.

The impact of what remains the worst peace-time disaster in British maritime history was devastating. Harris and Lewis had already lost another 1000 men during four years of war; a generation had been wiped out. Reporting the tragedy, the *Scotsman* noted: 'The villages of Lewis are like places of the dead. The homes of the island are full of lamentation – grief that cannot be comforted. Scarcely a family has escaped the loss of a near blood relative. Many have had sorrow heaped upon sorrow.'

Some of the bodies were never found. The scars ran deep. Survivors could not talk of the tragedy. Some felt guilt for having survived. Mass emigrations in the 1920s followed. A shadow fell on the islands, lasting for decades, never truly lifting, despite the last survivor dying in 1992.

'The blackness of that day still lingers,' Kenny said simply.

St Kilda was on my mind, specifically getting to St Kilda. For once, I had planned ahead, reserving a slot on a sailing to the archipelago a month earlier. I had booked on the basis that should the trip be cancelled, there would be a back-up day – in this case, the following day – as long as the weather had improved. My first opportunity to reach St Kilda had gone the same way as my ill-fated excursion to the Shiants, a victim of high seas. I was meant to be on the archipelago today. There was still tomorrow, the back-up day, however. My time had suddenly become pressed. I had no option of waiting a week for the low front to relinquish its hold on the islands. For the first time in three months, I was on a deadline. Today was Monday. In seven days' time I had to be on a flight from Inverness to London. My timeframe to reach St Kilda was narrowing.

I had repeated my steps of the previous morning, from Garenin to the churches in Carloway, and I was continuing along the main road to the village broch when a car pulled alongside. As the passenger door swung open, a voice shouted: 'Lift?' I jumped in.

Two men were sitting in the front seats. They were heading to Stornoway. Folk music blared from a stereo. I asked them to drop me off at Callanish, with the driver insisting he take me to the ancient standing stones in the village. As they pulled away, my mobile phone bleeped. I had a missed call and a voice message. It was from the cruise

192

company. I listened hopefully. It was bad news. St Kilda was off. The weather forecast was even worse tomorrow than today.

The Callanish stones are 4000 years old but were only discovered in 1857 when the surrounding peat was excavated. They are awe-inspiring, complex, ethereal – a microcosm of the Hebrides. While the stones of Stonehenge in Wiltshire are aligned to the sun, the alignment of Callanish relates to the astronomical observations of the moon. The setting of Callanish adds to its allure. Standing on the prow of a small hill, the view is remarkable: the rough outline of Great Bernera and its multitude of surrounding isles congregate to the west; a great tract of undulating wilderness punctuated by thousands of lochs rolls away to the south; the bleak moor and little hills of central Lewis extended to the north and east.

I moped about the site and then moped about the visitor centre, still dwelling on St Kilda. I watched tourists come and go: a coach party from Birmingham, a family from north-east England, five French women. At one point I am sure I saw Will Self, although he seemed to be speaking in a foreign language. I had not the heart to chase after him to check.

I eventually moved on, walking away from Callanish and onto the main road between Carloway and Stornoway. As cars approached from behind, I pushed my thumb out. I was ignored. Two hours earlier I had earned a lift in Carloway without even trying. I had not needed to ask. Now I was trying, adhering to hitchhiking etiquette, and I was failing miserably. If anything, cars seemed to accelerate as they swept past my right ear. Some twenty, maybe twenty-five cars zoomed by, each one amplifying my demoralisation and depression. Hearing another coming, I stuck out my arm. I heard the vehicle brake and slow. A lift at last, I rejoiced. I turned around to see an ambulance, the driver shaking his head. By this time I had walked two miles to Garynahine, where a road breaks off to the south towards Great Bernera and Uig. I continued along the main road, where the traffic would be heavier and my chances of gaining a lift greater. I had been going only another five minutes when a car miraculously pulled over. I ran towards it gleefully, tossed my rucksack into the boot and jumped in the passenger seat. The driver was a woman in her 40s, I reckoned, with curly blonde hair and a shirt that accentuated her generous cleavage. She lived on Great Bernera, the island I had admired earlier from Callanish. Her son would take me fishing on his creel boat, she offered enthusiastically.

I had already decided I would go where my lift was going, even if that meant Stornoway.

'Where are you heading?' she asked.

'Not sure,' I said, hesitating. 'How about you?'

'Stornoway.'

'Stornoway it is then,' I sighed.

As soon as I got to Stornoway, I wondered why I had come back. The solution was to leave as soon as possible. I had vital business to attend to before I could escape: checking the weather forecast. A woman at the tourist information centre delivered the outlook – Wednesday: heavy rain, force seven winds; Thursday: slightly better; Friday: sunny (honestly), force three winds; Saturday: even better. What the forecast gave no indication of was the sea swell. High winds had churned and tossed the sea for almost a fortnight. The swell would take time to drop, to settle. A sunny outlook meant nothing. Friday and Saturday seemed plausible St Kilda days, but if the swell had not subsided, the cruise ships would not leave the Long Island.

I walked to the bus station, ruminating on my next

destination. I could go to Uig and wait for the weather to clear, then I would be close to the embarkation point for St Kilda. But that would mean having to camp in this wild weather. I could stay in Stornoway, a possibility I quickly ruled out. I could go to Leverburgh or Tarbert, where I could attempt to find another trip to St Kilda, and in both places I would be able to find a hostel bed. Or I could go to Great Bernera and go out on my lift's son's creel boat in East Loch Roag. None of the options enthused me. The weather had squashed my fervour for adventure.

I would try my luck in Tarbert, I finally decided. I could always come back to Uig. Over the hills I went, exiting Lewis, entering Harris.

17

Harris

There are two seasons in Scotland: June and winter.
Billy Connolly

❦

So close but so far. That was Scarp.

Harris and Scarp are separated by the Sound of Scarp, a channel of water no more than 400 metres broad at its narrowest stretch. I was standing on Tràigh Mheilein, an empty, windswept strand overlooking the east coast of the mist-capped island. A finger of sand, pointing the way to Scarp, extended into the sound. A squadron of seagulls strutted about the shallows at the furthest reach of the digit, guarding the golden road into the waves.

Scarp – two miles broad, three miles long, rising to 308 metres at its highest point – is one of the so-called Atlantic outliers, a romantic list of islands at the very margins of the British Isles. The outliers – among them also the Flannan Islands, Gaisgear, the Monach Islands, North Rona, Rockall, St Kilda and Sula Sgeir – share a common, sad denominator: they have no permanent residents.

The proximity of Scarp to Harris meant it survived longer than the rest. The island was once home to more than 200 people. That was in the late 1880s. Less than a century later, Scarp was empty. Links with the mainland Western Isles were severed one-by-one in the 1960s until a 20th century existence became impossible. The school was closed, the post office shut, the Church of Scotland would not replace the lay preacher and the telephone line went down. All this was on an island where there was no electricity supply. There was a sad sense of inevitably about it all: the last permanent residents were relocated to Harris in 1971. A burial ground, a church and houses – they are no longer homes – stand above the eastern shore of Scarp, a deteriorating memorial of abandonment.

The Sound is Scarp is shallow. It is swimmable. But then so is the English Channel. I had contemplated such a feat – the Sound of Scarp, not the English Channel – ideally at low tide, when the distance between Harris and Scarp would be its shortest. It is possible, apparently, albeit highly dangerous, to wade between the islands. Lives have been lost in this pursuit. Gulf of Corryvreckan it is certainly not, but only when I stood on Tràigh Mheilein, gazing across the seething, swirling waters of the Sound of Scarp, did I appreciate the preposterousness of the notion of walking down the golden road and eventually reaching another island. It would be the last walk I would go on. Alone and without the assistance of a boat, I would certainly be swept away to my death. And then, even if I miraculously reached Scarp, how would I ever get back?

I walked to the northern end of Tràigh Mheilein and turned a corner, before climbing inland over the rippled contours of abandoned lazy beds. I soon attained the summit of a grassy hill, overlooking a small loch occupying a depression. Stretching away to the east was Loch Resort, a slit of water extending deep into Harris, the abandoned village of Kilochresort at the head of the sea loch. The outlook from the prow was as wild as I had seen on the islands: a moody sea and vast tracts of rocky, unliveable land. A single house, labelled as Crabhadail on my map,

197

stood on the far bank of the loch, occupying a fairytale setting. Two miles from the nearest road, the retreat was accessible only by mountain path or sea.

After circumnavigating the loch I was within 50 metres of the property when its occupant appeared proprietarily on the front doorstep. The man stared at me with unwarranted suspicion. I asked him if he owned the building. He nodded, folding his arms across his chest. I was not welcome here, that was clear. The man wanted his solitude back. Were I a millionaire, I would have offered to buy the home on the spot.

The track to Hushinish clung to the swampy edge of the loch, before sweeping upwards to a col, soon after joining a coastal path high above the Sound of Scarp. Much of the way was muddy and rough; the track intermittent. I marvelled at the efforts of the Crabhadail householder who must frequently have to undertake this journey to reach the nearest road, his link to civilisation. How did he get bulky items home? By boat, theoretically, but that still required the goods to be hauled some 500 metres cross-country from the shore of Loch Crabhadail. It was a mystery I would never answer.

Once off the coastal path I crossed machair meadows and reached a stone pier, the embarkation point for Scarp. I stood forlornly on the jetty, imagining a boat arriving to whisk me across the water. None came. Sheltering from an ever-increasing wind, I waited for a bus that would return me to Tarbert.

Tarbert was where I had spent the previous night, an angry, frustrating night. Never again, I had told myself in the morning. The cause of my ire was a Norwegian, a man who – in spite of his enormous bulk – had managed to propel himself all the way from Lochboisdale, 70 road miles to the south, by bicycle. My respect for him ends there. He was spandex-attired, as cyclists who treat their sport seriously tend to be. Some people suit spandex and some, bluntly, do not. The Norwegian fell into the latter category, a classic case. Not that he saw it like that. Rolls of fat spilled out from beneath his jersey. His shorts repeatedly slid down, revealing a fleshy backside. Loose on the waist, the shorts were tight on the crotch. I need not elaborate further. I stared at the grotesque figure, imagining the litres of sweat that had today soaked and then dried into the spandex. When bedtime arrived, it did not occur to him to change the clothes he had spent the day toiling in. Nor did he shower. Fate would have it he was sleeping in a neighbouring bunk to mine.

To be fair to the Norwegian, he was not alone in his offending. The dormitory was full, at least a dozen bodies in close – too close – proximity. A repugnant stench hung in the clammy air, a mishmash of feet, flatulence and sweat. The longer I lay in my bunk, unsleeping, the more I sensed a putrid miasma permeating my skin, infecting my innards, poisoning my lungs. I felt ill. At least three people were snoring too, the Norwegian easily the loudest. They snored unwittingly in unison and sometimes so loud that their own snorts awakened them. Yet – as it infuriatingly is with the snoring kind – they would return to sleep instantly. Others in the dormitory had the sense to evacuate. I heard them leave, but not come back. They presumably made beds for themselves in the corridors or the ground-floor lounge. Stubbornly, I had stayed where I was, rehearsing what I would do, where I would go, should I choose to join the evacuees. I thought about my second night on Rum. Was this worse? I thought about my second night on Barra. Was this worse? It was a hard call.

*

So I went to Rhenigidale instead, another Gatliff hostel, travelling along on a road that plunged, lurched, twisted and turned, before reaching a hamlet of around half a dozen homes at the mouth of Loch Seaforth. I whiled away the hours chain-drinking tea with Róisín, a physics teacher from Glasgow, talking mountains with Michael, a walker who had climbed almost two-thirds of the 1555 Marilyns – the list of British hills higher than 150 metres – and later drinking Laphroaig with three German travellers. I attempted to put thoughts of St Kilda to the back of my mind. It was only Tuesday. There was still time for the weather to improve, to 'blow itself out' as islanders speculated. But it was hard not think of the increasingly distant archipelago, for outside was tumultuous. Any hosteller brave enough to venture beyond the walls of the building returned with an expletive. All night rain peppered the windows and the wind groaned.

It was no better in the morning. I called the cruise company. The Friday sailing had already been cancelled, despite it only being Wednesday. The swell in the Atlantic would be too great in two days' time, even if the weather improved dramatically, I was told. My heart sank. St Kilda seemed as far away as America.

Róisín took pity on me, driving us to Tarbert. I pored over yet another weather outlook at yet another tourist information centre. The forecast for Friday gave cause for confidence. 'Sunny', it said. But the winds would be strong, force five, hence the cancellation. The outlook for Saturday – the last possible day I could travel to St Kilda – had worsened markedly, although the meteorologists were maddeningly vague: 'sun, mist and rain.' The Atlantic depression was 'slow-moving', apparently.

A trio of cruise companies ran excursions to St Kilda, meaning I clung to a whisker of hope that one or both of the others may be sailing on Friday. These voyages departed from Leverburgh, while the company that had twice cancelled my ill-fated expedition would have set forth from Uig, a harder, longer crossing to St Kilda, I had been told. Imploring brutal honesty, I asked an assistant at the centre what she reckoned the likelihood of boats, any boat, advancing to the archipelago on Friday. Either all the cruises would go or none would go, the woman replied, in a few seconds effectively extinguishing my aspirations of gaining St Kilda.

I gave up. I could see no alternative. If I could not cross 400 metres of sea to Scarp, how could I breach 40 miles of ocean to St Kilda? Besides, I am a landlubber. The thought of being at sea on a boat tottering in towering water, filled me with dread. Part of me was relieved. I need no longer obsess over St Kilda. If only it was that easy. Still, I began to make plans to leave Harris the following day, Thursday. I would travel to Skye. An annual hill race on Glamaig – a 775-metre scree-smothered mountain overlooking Loch Sligachan – was being held on Saturday. I would compete in the race ahead of returning to Inverness.

I spent the day with Róisín and Anna, her travelling partner, touring Harris by the comfort of car. I was glad of the company. We motored south, stopping at Luskentyre to walk across a white-sand beach, vast and windblown. Taransay, the setting of the year-long reality series, *Castaway 2000*, rose in the distance, a mile offshore. On we went, along a coast-clinging road, whizzing past more sandy beaches lashed by white waves, before turning south-east to reach Leverburgh. We ate soup with warm bread three miles further up the road in Rodel, at a hotel facing a pretty harbour where seals frolicked in the surf. Replenished, we travelled north along the Golden Road, so called, apparently, because of the exorbitant cost of creating such a route amid an undulating, wild landscape of loch, moor and rock. The route twisted in and out, up and down, overlooking the fjord-like fringe of east Harris, passing through strung out hamlets with Gaelic or Viking names: Fionnsabhagh, Fleoideabhagh, Geocrab, Plocrapol. Torrential rain began to fall as we reached Tarbert. We swept through without stopping, returning to Rhenigidale. Róisín put the kettle on.

The weather was better. The sky was overcast, but the wind had dropped. So much so that I took a run up Todun, a 522-metre hill overlooking Rhenigidale, made slippery by the rain. A tin box wedged between two rocks in the summit cairn contained a visitor's book and pen. I added my observations and descended sharply to the hostel for breakfast.

Róisín again drove us to Tarbert. The tourist information centre, inevitably, was my first of port of call, by habit rather than in hope. The weather forecast for the current day and the next four days was typically posted on the inside of the glass door facing out. Today another notice caught my attention before the forecast: a trip to the Shiant Islands, leaving Tarbert today at midday – in 15 minutes time. I thought hard about the prospect. It was not cheap, but surely worth it, I reasoned, especially in light of my failure to reach St Kilda. I was mulling over my options when a further bill caught my eye. The words on the sheet ordered themselves in my brain like a hallucination. It was an announcement of a trip to St Kilda, leaving tomorrow, Friday, the day when the swell was meant to be too great. At the bottom of the advertisement were two magic words: 'places available.'

There might not be any left, I decided instantly, excitement draining into an expectation of disappointment. It was best not to get my hopes up, I thought. I did not know how long the advert had been up. It was not as if I was the only person seeking to reach St Kilda. Numerous excursions to the archipelago had been cancelled; many of them would be seeking alternative expeditions. Still, I scrawled down the landline number on the poster and ran to the nearest pay phone, cursing the loss of my mobile, which had stopped working on the day of my second visit to Stornoway. The line rang and rang and rang. But there was no answer. I scurried back to the tourist centre, took down the mobile phone number and returned to the booth. This time, Angus Campbell, the skipper-boss of Kilda Cruises, answered. His voice was raised, wind whistling down the receiver.

'I'm on my way to the Shiants,' he said.

Each word was fainter than the last, before there was silence at the other end of the line. After 10 seconds of nothing I suddenly heard his voice loud and clear. There were still places available, he said. I jumped for joy in the box. St Kilda was feasible, a goer, provided the weather forecast – favourable at present – did not become unfavourable.

'Call me at seven,' Angus said, 'when I'll know what's happening.'

I had waited seven days to find out if I was to go to St Kilda. I could wait another seven hours.

Róisín and Anna had already left. I wanted to tell someone, but I was alone again. The cruise would leave from Leverburgh, so I gathered my belongings and made my way south, breaking the journey at Northton (Taobh Tuath, the village's Gaelic name, has greater appeal). I began to walk towards the imposing mass of Ceapabhal, but was turned back by rain before I had even reached the ramparts of the hill. With a bus to Leverburgh not due for an hour, I called in at the Western Isles' genealogy research centre, a place with an exclamation mark – Seallam!

The most startling aspect of Seallam! (which is genuinely worthy of an exclamation mark) is a map charting where in the world emigrants from the Western Isles eventually re-settled. Tens of thousands of people were forced from their island homes during the Clearances, but emigration, albeit optional, continues today, with population decline caused by young people preferring to live, study and work on the Scottish mainland. Hundreds of emigrants went to Australia, Canada and the US, but others sought obscurer climes – Jamaica, Iceland, St Helena, Sierra Leone and South Korea. It was only when I stood before the map that I appreciated the extent to which the blood of islanders is sprinkled about the globe.

I camped for the first time since being blown about on Barra, retreating to a sheltered slope of Roineabhal; open ground close to Leverburgh pier was too exposed to the wind. I had contemplated another night in a hostel, but I deemed that if camping was implausible, then so was sailing to St Kilda.

With the tent pitched, I brought a pan of pasta to the boil. I flipped over the pan to drain the pasta. Disaster: the lid popped open, penne thrown to the earth. Picking grass out of the food, I did not bother to add sauce and ate the pasta from where it had fallen. I had forgotten the simple joys of camping.

Finding a red phone box, I called Angus a little after the assigned hour. I was worried; the wind did not seem to have abated. It was a task to even open the door of the booth, such was the frenetic insistence of the gusts. Once inside, I feared I would never get out. It did not seem to matter. Angus delivered the news I craved; I was going to St Kilda.

I lay in my tent fantasising about the distant islands, imagining the surrounding sea becalmed. It was no longer wishful thinking.

18

St Kilda

The inhabitants of St Kilda are much happier than the generality of Mankind, being almost the only People in the World who feel the Sweetness of true Liberty.

Martin Martin, 1697

♧

Scouring the horizon, again and again, concentrating, eyes aching, scarcely allowing lids to blink. Where was St Kilda?

And then an unashamedly excited outburst, a land ahoy moment: 'There it is, there it is.' 'It' was Boreray, the second-largest of the St Kilda isles, climbing cathedral-like, jagged and forbidding, hundreds of metres high, from the greyness of the mighty Atlantic. Stac an Armin, a fearsome fang of rock, tilted like a monstrous leaning tower, emerged next, appearing off the northern prow of Boreray. The farthest-flung of all of the British islands, the islands at the edge of the world, were gloriously revealing themselves. St Kilda existed, St Kilda was real. The shapes of these islands, slight and indistinct at first, grew by the moment, becoming larger and larger, swelling to gigantic, fearful proportions. Another sea pillar, Stac Lee, the molar to the incisor of Stac an Armin, came into sight, then Hirta, the largest of the islands and our destination, its haunches sheer, its head lost in cloud.

If islands are a metaphor for the world, St Kilda is a metaphor for humanity: its frailty and its strength, but

206

most of all its ability to self-destruct. This once Utopian, untainted archipelago of astonishing grandeur, and inhabited for more than 2000 years, was evacuated in 1930. The government was inundated with requests from people wanting to replace the 36 displaced St Kildans. Sir Reginald MacLeod of MacLeod, the proprietor of St Kilda, and the Scottish Office, rejected them all. 'It would be folly to remove one lot of people who know the island and replace them with a group of strangers,' Sir Reginald insisted. So human life on St Kilda ceased.

Disaster, disease and emigration, and subsequent re-population, caused the number of St Kildans to fluctuate between 30 and 180 from the late 17th century to 1930. Little is known of life on the islands before 1697, the year Martin Martin, a well-to-do writer native to the Trotternish peninsula on Skye, spent three weeks living on the archipelago. In his book on the islands, *A Late Voyage to St Kilda*, Martin described an idyllic place, where the air was 'sharp and wholesome' and the hills were 'often covered with ambient white mists'. But he also wrote of a savage, inhuman place: 'The inhabitants live together in a little village, which carries all the signs of an extream poverty; the houses are of a low form, having all the doors to the northeast, both on purpose to secure them from the shocks of the tempest of the south-west winds.' It is this juxtaposition of St Kilda – at times heavenly, at times hellish – that would captivate travellers and tourists for centuries.

Martin described a social anomaly, an island nation evolving without interference from the rest of the world. Tom Steel, writing in *The Life and Death of St Kilda*, remarked the islanders had more in common with the inhabitants of the south Atlantic Ocean island of Tristan da Cunha than the people of Edinburgh or Glasgow. The archipelago was considered so remote that when James IV of Scotland decreed all islands were under his command, St Kilda was omitted from his kingdom because it was too far away for him to provide protection. World affairs passed St Kildans by. News of the death of William IV and the coronation of Queen Victoria did not filter through to the St Kildans until 1838 – a year after the events took place. Writing in 1819, the scientist John MacCulloch declared: 'Safe in its own whirlwinds and cradled in its own tempests, it heeds not the storms which shake the foundations of Europe.' The world of the St Kildans was their archipelago, its beginning and end.

Despite the surroundings of fish-filled waters, the islanders looked to the sky for sustenance. Seabirds provided St Kildans with much of what they needed to survive: eggs and meat for nourishment, feathers and skins for clothing, oil for light, medicine for wellbeing and fertiliser for the fields. The birds later became a source of income, with island plumiers supplying London fashion houses and the military with dress accessories – a trade that suffered as fashions changed.

Gannets formed the staple diet of the St Kildans until the mid-18th century, but hunting missions to the nests of these birds were complicated by their distance from the archipelago's centre of population. Open rowing boats were used to transport the St Kildans, who could not swim, to the uninhabited islands of Boreray, Stac an Armin and Stac Lee, separated from Hirta by a four-mile tract of treacherous sea. Of the many disasters at sea, the loss of 18 men returning from Uist with seed corn was among the worst.

A change in eating habits was significant, for fulmars – the new bird of choice – nested on Hirta, enabling (theoretically) less dangerous and shorter hunting expeditions. The bird was seen as so integral to the self-sufficiency of the people that the Reverend Kenneth Macaulay remarked in

1758: 'Deprive us of the fulmar, and St Kilda is no more.' Even in 1875, fulmars were critical to the survival of St Kilda. More than 9000 birds were caught in that year – the equivalent of 126 birds each for the 72 inhabitants.

Whether seabirds were hunted on Boreray, Hirta or the precipitous stacks, the slaying missions were fraught with peril. Astonished by the climbing feats he witnessed, Martin wrote: 'The inhabitants, I must tell you, run no small danger in the quest of the fowls and eggs, insomuch that I fear it would be thought an hyperbole to relate the inaccessibleness, steepness, and height, of those formidable rocks which they venture to climb. I myself have seen some of them climb up the corner of a rock with their backs to it, making use only of their heels and elbows, without any other assistance; and they have this way acquired a dexterity in climbing beyond any I ever yet saw; necessity has made them apply themselves to this, and custom has perfected them in it; so that it is become familiar to them almost from their cradles, the young boys of three years old being to climb the walls of their houses: their frequent discourses of climbing, together with the fatal end of several in the exercise of it, is the same to them, as that of fighting and killing is with soldiers, and so is become as familiar and less formidable to them, than otherwise certainly it would be.'

As Martin observed, the St Kildan man had an innate ability to climb, and their bodies adapted to the demands of their sport. Steel explained: 'The bone structure of their ankles differed from that of people born elsewhere. The ankle of a St Kildan male was practically half as thick again as that of a mainland person, and the toes were set further apart and almost prehensile.'

The nature of the hunting grounds and the islanders' rudimentary equipment meant survival depended on skill,

and often simply on luck. One story told by Charles
Maclean in his 1972 biography of St Kilda, *Island on
the Edge of the World*, describes two cragsmen descending
a cliff on the same rope. The man highest up noticed the
rope was fraying. He had a Touching the Void-style choice
to make. Do nothing and they would both perish on the
rocks beneath. Or cut the rope, meaning he would save
himself but send his friend to certain doom. He chose
survival, cutting the rope beneath his feet and scrambling
to safety before the cord above him snapped.

Sustainability: an often vacuous buzzword spouted by
developers, town planners and politicians. When associated
with communities of people, it literally means the capacity
to support life. Was life on St Kilda sustainable? For two
millennia, it undoubtedly was. The archipelago's survival as
a place of human habitation is evidence of that. St Kildans
did not need the outside world; they were self-sufficient.

But the curious outside world came to St Kilda, and that
world brought trouble.

When the first steamship, *Vulcan*, arrived in Village Bay
in 1838 packed with tourists, the watching St Kildans fled
to the high hills at the alien sound of a brass brand striking
up. Realising there was money to be made from these
novelty-seekers, however, islanders soon overcame their
anxieties. By the end of the century the red carpet was
being rolled out to visiting ships. The woman would line up
on the shore, preparing their wares of eggs, stuffed birds,
tweed, woollens and other souvenirs for sale, while the men
would row out to meet the newly-arrived vessel. The
visitors came to St Kilda to feel, see and touch what the
archipelago represented – freedom, isolation and wildness –
but in doing so, they were robbing the islands of what they
came to seek. The St Kildans became to be regarded as

circus freaks or 'wild animals at the zoo', one observer wrote. The traditional way of life was dying.

Physically, St Kilda was unaltered. It was the attitude of the people that changed, making life on St Kilda increasingly unsustainable. Ignorance of the outside world meant they survived in an undisturbed bubble. Every deed, every action, every slaughtered bird, was for the benefit of the community. By the early 20th century, the St Kildans had lost the common purpose that had bonded generations of islanders for hundreds of years. The people had heard of greener grass. Utopia had been smashed. The St Kildans 'ceased to believe in themselves; they relinquished their responsibility to survive and left the matter in the hands of fate', Maclean lamented.

The opening of a post office, a school and, critically, the construction of a pier in Village Bay to boost the fishing industry, failed to stem the decline. The post office was dependent on passing Fleetwood trawlers to secure delivery; the school could do little for children beyond primary education; and even if the islanders had surplus fish, there was no means of export to the mainland. Handouts became increasingly common. Evacuation was first mooted in 1912 due to apparent food shortages, but the outbreak of war in Europe two years later quelled the debate. The downward spiral accelerated after the conflict, with the population plunging from 73 in 1920 to 37 in 1928.

St Kilda's destiny seemed decided, for those years were dogged by bad tidings: the Scottish Office's rejection of a proposal for a regular steamship service between the Hebrides and the archipelago, deaths outstripping births, emigration, illness, poor harvests and depression. Those who left the island were chiefly young men, the able-bodied, the people who should have represented St Kilda's future. Then, early in 1930, a St Kildan woman became ill with

211

appendicitis. The remoteness of St Kilda meant it was several weeks before she could be transported to a hospital in Glasgow. It was too late; Mary Gillies died. It was the final straw.

That spring the 36 residents all signed a petition that was sent to the Secretary of State for Scotland imploring evacuation. On August 28, 1930, they got their wish. Abandoning their homes, the soon to be ex-islanders boarded *Harebell* and sailed away from St Kilda, some with tears in their eyes, others with relief in their hearts.

There were nine of us aboard the St Kilda-bound cruiser: a motley troupe of artists, photographers, walkers and writers, with a secondary school teacher and an islomaniac – a traveller on a mission to visit as many of the British islands as possible – supplementing the ranks. Angus sat at the ship's wheel, his eyes focused on the rolling ocean ahead. There was one other member of crew, whose job it had been to issue life jackets as we left Leverburgh. The rest of us, except for the islomaniac, oddly enough, congregated on wooden benches on the deck, gazing out to sea and craning necks to follow the flight of birds. Once sat down it was best to stay sat down; every time I released my grip of any surface attached to the cruiser, I felt sure the bobbing, trembling motion of our passage would fling me overboard.

We fizzed along the Sound of Harris, slipping past the eastern rims of Pabbay and Shillay, the swell growing as we escaped the shelter of the channel. As the boat began cutting a route through these waters, the necessity of sick bags on the expedition to St Kilda became evident. Our passage was akin to a fairground ride, a stomach-churning one that would last three hours. Endlessly we scaled peaks and sunk into troughs; up and down, up and down, again and again and again. I longed for tranquility, for the sea to settle and flatten.

Looking from face to face, I speculated who among the passengers would be the first to succumb to motion sickness. Not the English artist. His mettle was in no doubt: he had been to St Kilda before, becoming stranded by a storm for five days and living off beans and canned fish. Not the Dutch photographer. When he walked across the deck he did so with poise, unlike the rest of us who stumbled like drunks. Nor the teacher. She was from Stornoway, a Hebridean lassie made of sturdy stuff. And surely not the islomaniac? A passenger on so many boats and ferries, the passage to St Kilda did not seem to interest him. Then it struck me – if anyone was likely to vomit, it was I. It was an unwelcome revelation, one I feared would become a self-fulfilling prophecy. The prospect of imminent heaving, and the associated embarrassment, was now rooted in my mind. Sitting an arm's length from the Atlantic swell it was hard to overcome such nauseous thoughts.

I tried, but when I should have been dwelling on fine reflections of the Hebrides, I was meditating on being sick, specifically on the logistics of whether to vomit into a bag or directly into the sea. Unwittingly, Angus distracted me from this dilemma. He abruptly cut power to the engine. Taking the place of the growl was an uneasy silence. The ocean seemed calm and composed for a moment. But it was merely a moment, for in the next the boat was no longer travelling forwards. It was travelling upwards. A tremendous slap thumped the bow as the vessel crested a tremendous wave, before plunging into its deep trough. Lifted off my seat by the impact, I pushed myself into a corner, wrapping my fingers around the slats on my section of bench. I held on for dear life; I could think of few worse prospects than swimming in this sea.

'Rogue wave,' Angus shouted unfazed, as the engine roared back into life.

It was enough to make a man empty his porridge into the Atlantic.

We had continued for a short time when the engine was cut again. We waited, braced for another wave. Yet none came. Side to side the ship swayed, 11 souls at the whim of nature. Silence took hold again, accentuating the smallness, the insignificance, of our existence among the vastness of a great ocean. Angus's crewman came rushing out of the covered section of the vessel, pointing to the sea. Our eyes followed his hand. Dorsal fins, two of them. We stood still, mesmerised, soundless. The sharks approached our vessel until they were close enough for us to see the tremendous bulk of their bodies under the water, their gaping mouths. The creatures veered sharply towards the stern of the boat, slipping out of sight beneath the waves, before their dorsal fins re-appeared several metres away. Seconds later they vanished again, as if they had been beckoned to another place.

Our journey was coming to an end; the swell was subsiding. The 60-million-year-old cliffs of Hirta reared skywards, impossibly high and steep. Seabirds swept overhead, forming a guard of honour. As Angus negotiated the cruiser around the south-eastern fringe of the island, Village Bay, the only safe landing point, came into view. Above the seashore was what we had all come to see: The Village, a line of roofless, stone buildings that were once the dwellings of St Kildans, the place where civilisation on this extraordinary island was carried out.

The simple elegance of The Village and the drama of the surrounding hills were glaringly contrasted by a block of Ministry of Defence Nissen huts. The military has had a presence on St Kilda since the 1950s. A radar station tracks missiles fired from a test range on Benbecula. Not only does such an operation require the ugly paraphernalia of a radar station, topped by what has the appearance of a gigantic golf ball, on Mullach Mòr, but also living quarters for staff who oversee the workings. There is a pub too, the appropriately-named Puff Inn. The attendance of the military on St Kilda is both incongruous and ironic; the island left empty because it lacked the infrastructure to support a population now has the necessary workings – a public water supply, electricity – and round-the-clock communication with the rest of the UK to sustain a permanent population. 'If only the St Kildans had managed to hang on for another 30 years,' the scientist John Love has speculated, 'they would have been astonished at the services that have developed since the Army arrived in 1957! In which case the evacuation may never have occurred.'

We were taken by tender to a concrete pier, watched over by several morose contractors, standing idly as if they had forgotten what they were meant to be doing, before being met by the island's National Trust for Scotland warden. The warden relayed a brief history of St Kilda: its hundreds of years of habitation, the evacuation, of course, and the subsequent stewardship of the conservation body. The introduction was scarcely necessary. Few people travel to St Kilda knowing nothing of its history and significance.

The archipelago is a double World Heritage Site, the only one of its kind in the UK. UNESCO inscribed the archipelago as a natural World Heritage Site in 1984 and then as a cultural one in 2005. The recognition elevated St Kilda to dual status, joining an elite band of just 24 global locations, including Ayers Rock in Australia, Machu Picchu in Peru and Mount Athos in Greece, which share similar acclaim.

The Nissen huts, a row of fuel tanks and the radar station aside, the natural charms of this volcanic archipelago are immediately apparent: a landscape so extraordinarily carved it seems a benevolent creator lingered longer here, some of the highest sea cliffs in Europe and vast colonies of crying, circling seabirds.

Our group of nine split up, going our separate ways. The hill-walker marched off in determined fashion towards Conachair, the island's highest point. The teacher ran into the arms of her boyfriend who was working on the island. She had not seen him for a month. I could well imagine what the next minutes held in store for them. Three others – the arty brigade, I dubbed them – loitered about the pier; Angus was later to take them on a circumnavigation of Hirta. The rest of us wandered away from the pier in the general direction of The Village, not knowing quite what to do now we were here. I made for the east end of what one could call 'urban Hirta' where I found a mounted gun pointing out to Village Bay. The gun was put here in 1918 after Hirta was attacked by a German submarine, but was never fired.

There are umpteen thoroughfares named Main Street in the British Isles, though no other is quite like Hirta's Main Street. This grassy road passes through The Village, with all the homes lining up on the northern side of the track, crofting land sloping seawards to the south. It is a road that witnessed the life and death of St Kilda. I walked in heavy rain, conscious of not wanting to waste a moment. Sheltering in the kirk or the schoolroom would have meant wasting moments, however cold and wet I became. Half a dozen of the houses had been reroofed and restored, of which one had been converted into a little museum. But the vast majority of the buildings were lifeless, with floors overgrown and covered by droppings. Eight decades of Atlantic weather had ravaged these places until they had become homes fit only for sheep. To the east of what is known as house five is the building that once contained the island's post office, now also a ruin. This is where the so-called St Kilda parliament – made up of all able-bodied men on the island – would meet daily to decide what work needed to be done on the island.

Alone and with my back to the huts, I could imagine what life might have looked like on Hirta, and I was over-whelmed by the remoteness of such a life. Had I travelled directly to St Kilda from Edinburgh or London, that sense of remoteness would have been heightened still further. After three months of island-hopping, I was conditioned to lands surrounded by water. I had grown familiar with the sensation of being isolated from the rest of the world. But my notion of remoteness had constantly been redefined. Arran seemed remote in comparison with mainland Ayr-shire, but I ridiculed such a notion when I visited Colonsay and Jura. Coll, in particular, and Tiree, had seemed further isolated still, more Outer Hebrides than Inner, as had Rum. St Kilda took my definition of isolation and remoteness to new levels. This was the edge – a geographical edge standing at the frontier of north-west Europe, but also a cultural and social edge.

And the most extraordinary concept of all: people – hundreds of them – had lived on this island for centuries, a happy, organised, fulfilled, thriving community 40 miles from the next nearest humans and 110 miles from the Scottish mainland. St Kilda is so remote that it is nearer Rockall, an islet on the edge of the European continental shelf, than its capital, Edinburgh. Sharing a longitude with Portugal, the archipelago is so distant from the rest of Britain that the islands are either ignored by mapmakers or relegated to an inset. It is little wonder then that St Kilda is known as the island group at the edge of the world.

I succumbed to shelter; the rain was now torrential. Thinking of the unfortunate hill-walker, I made a beeline for the museum. The visitors' book revealed we were the first to come ashore for 11 days, a mark of how bad the weather had been. The comments were what one might expect, such is the aura of St Kilda: 'As awe-inspiring as I imagined'; 'hauntingly beautiful;' 'a world lost in time;' and a writer who had borrowed an appropriate line from the *Canadian Boat Song*: 'We in dreams behold the Hebrides.'

With the rain subsiding, I continued along Main Street, the houses becoming increasingly straggled and weather-beaten at this western end. Soon there were no more dwellings and I crossed a soggy field to reach a military road. Climbing upwards in a series of hairpins, the road starts at sea level and culminates on the 355-metre summit of Mullach Mòr. The route passed numerous cleits – stone-walled, grass-roofed huts used to store meat and turf – built in vast quantities by the St Kildans. The benefit of increasing altitude revealed dozens of these structures scattered across the floor of the glen. Standing resolutely against the on-slaught of wild weather, the cleits symbolise the resource-fulness of the St Kildans, who built more than 2000, including some on the precipitous stacks.

I was now on Mullach Mòr, a place dominated by the radar station. But it was from here that the shuddering stateliness of Hirta becomes apparent. The northern rim of Hirta fell away beneath my feet, cliffs dropping hundreds of metres to the ocean. The way ahead was pathless across squelchy bog, dropping to a tarn before rising abruptly to Conachair. Reaching the lochan, I met the walker. Un-daunted by the cloudburst, she had summited Conachair and was on her way back down. Seeing me, however, she

decided to ascend the mountain again, such was her pleasure in climbing it the first time.

We walked together for a minute, then I forged ahead, my
pace quickening as the gradient softened and the summit
grew closer. The highest point was an innocuous grassy
plateau, marked by a stone cairn. From here, I surveyed the
world, the edge of the sea. There was no mist to obscure the
wonders. Rain-heavy clouds were marching eastwards to
the Long Island. The woman arrived, panting but exultant.
A watery sun shone on us. I laughed aloud, a laugh of pure
astonishment, such was the glory of this place. As Maclean
testified, glimpsed from Conachair the ocean 'looks the way
it does from an aeroplane, without movement, unreal'. I felt
like I had on the ship during those moments before we
glimpsed the shark, humbled by the enormity of all around
me, humbled by my miniscule size in comparison to it.

As I looked across silvery waters to Boreray, I was
reminded of the words of Norman Heathcote, a late
19th century visitor to St Kilda. 'Pretty?' he wrote. 'No!
It's grand and awe-inspiring, but not pretty.' Indeed, it was
the grandest, most awe-inspiring view I had ever fixed my
eyes on. In the next instant, I recalled once being at the Iron
Age hill fort of Old Sarum, overlooking the Avon valley
north of Salisbury, when a large lady sidled up next to Fi
and I and gaped in a ridiculously exaggerated Canadian
twang: 'This . . . view . . . is . . . incredible!' She called over
her husband. 'Look at this! This view is incredible!' She
turned to Fi and I, repeating for a third time: 'This view is
incredible!' We would repeat 'incredible' hundreds more
times ourselves over the years, with the adjective becoming
an ironic byword for something that was the opposite to
'incredible'.

Yet St Kilda was incredible – incredible without the
quotation marks.

In a flurry of photograph-taking I had not noticed the hill-walker leave. Peering over the brow of the hill, I saw her negotiating her way downhill, following the same route we had earlier climbed up. Wanting to descend alone, but knowing I would soon catch her up and be drawn into conversation, I advanced instead on a direct approach to The Village, on a route that would bypass Mullach Mòr and the military road. I was watching my feet on the steep, grassy descent when I sensed a creature from the sky hurtling towards me, the sudden movement creating a whoosh of wind. Moments later, another whoosh, and another. I had become a target for bonxies. The warden had warned us about them. Bonxies are the nickname for great skuas, a relative newcomer to St Kilda having first bred here in 1963. The birds are combative and territorial – and I was in their territory. They have been known to attack humans, drawing blood on occasions. I imagined their beaks and claws, arriving at terrific speed, could do serious damage to a human head. The birds typically hone in on the highest point of its target. The warden advised us to use sticks, walking poles or an umbrella to fend them off.

I was unarmed. My highest point being my head, I resorted to putting my hands over my scalp and throwing myself to the ground every time I heard the now familiar sound of a dive-bombing bonxie. After a dozen or so failed attempts, I realised the bonxies always stopped short of striking me, and – becoming increasingly fearless – I taunted them to come, dallying down the slippery slope in an exaggerated zigzag. Once I understood their modus operandi, I was able to watch them in action. They would soar horizontally and seemingly innocently, before darting in my direction, lunging upwards again at the last moment.

The attacks slowed, then ceased; I was out of enemy territory. Running down the now gentler slope, I soon reached the head dyke of The Village, a wall originally designed to keep sheep away from homes, and regained Main Street, now bathed in sunlight. Walking down to the shore, I sat alone on the edge of a slipway, watching the tide gently lap the concrete. At the top of the slipway was a little, square building, with two or three seats and a table occupying the tiny space of floor. A sign outside said: 'Welcome to St Kilda International Sea and Airport Lounge.'

I could hear voices. My short time on Hirta was coming to an end. I was overwhelmed with sadness, not only for St Kilda, but for myself. My island adventure was almost over. I sauntered across to the others. The ranger had opened a little shop selling St Kilda-related souvenirs. I was hesitant to even go inside. It was trinket-buying tourists who helped to destroy St Kilda. Was I just as bad, a travelling voyeur wanting to tick St Kilda off my list of must-visit destinations? I clearly did not deem myself so awful, as I bought a postcard, scrawled some lines and addressed it to Fi in London, knowing I would probably beat the card home.

The boat rolled out of Village Bay. I looked back at Main Street and The Village, turned my eyes upwards to Conachair, wondering when, if ever, I would return. The cruiser gradually increased speed and bumped across a now lustrous sea to Boreray and the stacks. Hirta began to shrink in our wake. Sitting on the port side, my view of Stac Lee had been blocked for several minutes. I got up, motioning to change sides, but the Dutchman ushered me to sit again.

'Stay where you are,' he said cryptically, 'you're in the best place.'

Just then, Angus turned the boat on its side, so the port outlook now faced the direction we had been travelling. The view was a revelation. Stac Lee, colossal and smeared in guano, a titanic cliff adrift in the ocean, rose before us.

221

Countless gannets glided effortlessly over the stack, like midges swarming around a human head. Together, Boreray, Stac an Armin and Stac Lee are the breeding ground for the world's largest gannet colony, numbering some 30,000 pairs. The stack was a forbidding sight. Heathcote's words came to mind again: 'Grand and awe-inspiring.'

After sailing in these waters in 1879, the yachtsman R.A. Smith wrote: 'Had it been a land of demons, it could not have appeared more dreadful, and had we not heard of it before, we should have said that, if inhabited, it must be monsters.'

A mile on, we came to Stac an Armin, fiercer, leaner and loftier than Stac Lee. Here was another place worthy of monsters. Soaring to a height of 191 metres and plunging a further 100 metres beneath the waves, Stac an Armin is the highest sea stack in the UK. The sides of the needle breaking the water were black and devilishly steep, often vertical. Landing a boat here or manoeuvring one as close as possible to enable those onboard to fling themselves onto the stack seemed implausible, a suicidal undertaking. The Gaelic translation of Stac an Armin – stack of the soldier or warrior – could not have been more apt. Yet St Kildans regularly went ashore here, hunting and building cleits. We slipped silently through the narrow, rock-strewn channel separating Boreray and Stac an Armin until we were positioned beneath the 'overhang', a shadowy place where no sunlight pervaded.

'Keep your mouth closed,' someone shouted, as the boat slid under the rock. Guano fell on the deck like rain. The cry of birds was cacophonous, the stench, a foul mix of guano and rotting fish, overpowering.

It was unfathomable that people could live on Stac on Armin. There seemed to be no shelter, no surface that was horizontal. Yet a group of St Kildans had somehow inhabited the stack for the best part of a year. They were not there by choice.

The group – three men and eight boys – had been deposited on Stac an Armin for a fowling mission in the summer of 1727. Such visitations to the gannet colony were regular occurrences and the group would have arranged to be returned to Hirta with the fruits of their labour several days later. Only no boat came. The men and boys waited. A week went by, then a month, then six months, and still no boat. The group had no vessel of their own. As on the rest of St Kilda, Stac an Armin was treeless; they could not craft their own boat. There was no way of breaching the four-mile chasm between Stac and Armin and Hirta. Swimming – even if they could – would be a death sentence. Even the possibility of relocating to better-resourced Boreray, a crossing of little more than 200 metres was made hopeless by the sheer cliffs of the larger island. The group were stranded, marooned, and Stac an Armin is no desert island.

One can only speculate on the thoughts they dwelt on. They would not have been able to comprehend the reason for their mass abandonment. What about the prospect of the coming winter? Storms that engulfed St Kilda were dreadful to endure for those who had battened down the hatches in the relative shelter of The Village. A former islander described one storm as leaving the people 'deaf for a week'. Mary Cameron said: 'The noise of the wind, the pounding of the sea, were indescribable. This storm was accompanied by thunder and lightning, but we could often not hear the thunder for the other sounds.' The horror of countless storms lashing their rock-home, the torture of the Scottish winter, is unimaginable. Prisoners on this dreadful fang of rock, their lives were surely of abject misery.

Yet they endured. The desperate eleven drank from the stack's fresh water supply and ate birds, eggs and fish.

Writing of the group's experiences on the stack, Neil Mackenzie, the island minister from 1829 to 1843, noted: 'They lived on fish and fowls, but at times suffered much from cold and hunger. They made fish hooks out of a few rusty nails, and also contrived to stitch together their clothing with feathers and patch them with the skins of birds.'

Somehow they retained hope, somehow they survived the winter. Hope was rewarded; salvation came.

The group was rescued on May 13, 1728, nine months after being stranded, the steward of St Kilda their saviour. Returning to Hirta, they discovered the grim truth of why a boat had never come back. In their absence the island had been devastated by smallpox, brought to Hirta in the contaminated clothes of a St Kildan who had died of the disease during a visit to Harris. The aged man's relatives had retrieved his clothes, not knowing they harboured the deadly infection. The hunters had left the island before the plague strangled the island, sweeping from home to home, from islander to islander. The survivors had not forgotten about the men; there were simply too few able-bodied sailors to row the island's boat to Stac an Armin. So, ironically, what must have been a godforsaken existence on the stack, their nine-month imprisonment saved them from an even worse fate – almost certain death – had they remained on Hirta. The population of St Kilda had stood at 180 in 1697. On the group's homecoming, only four adults and 26 children – all of them orphans – were alive, with the epidemic thought to have wiped out 80 to 90 per cent of St Kilda's entire population.

Despite their near-death experiences on Stac an Armin, St Kildans continued to return to the monolith to collect birds and eggs. On one of the visits in 1840, fowlers made an unwitting contribution to the annals of British natural history by slaughtering the country's last native great auk. Believing the bird to be a witch, the superstitious St Kildans beat it to death with stones. By 1852 the great auk was extinct.

High on the south side of Stac an Armin was a bothy. Climbers who ascended Stac an Armin in the 1990s described this bothy as being able to seat up to 15 men, as well as being free-standing and larger than a hut on neighbouring Stac Lee. From the deck it was possible to see the entrance, appearing as a dark hole disappearing into bare rock. This bothy was once called home: the crude and paltry shelter of three men and eight boys for nine long months. It was also the place where the last great auk in the British Isles was imprisoned for three days before being stoned to death.

Much has been written and published on St Kilda. Writers find the archipelago an irresistible subject. Indeed, a book could be devoted exclusively to Stac an Armin, an island that stands as a marker for all of St Kilda, representing bravery, fortitude and perseverance, but also hardship, misunderstanding and, ultimately, profound sorrow.

Angus turned the boat to Harris. The outline of the archipelago grew hazy, becoming fainter and fainter. Then the islands were gone, swallowed up by the horizon, as if they had never existed. I went into one world, St Kilda faded into another. I felt a connection – a brief yet deep physical link – sever, but I knew the emotional bond, the stronger connection, would be lifelong.

19

Homeward

The whole object of travel is not to set foot on foreign land;
it is at last to set foot in one's own country as a foreign land.

G.K. Chesterton

☙

Life on Harris was mundane after St Kilda. I feared life
anywhere might be mundane after St Kilda.

I camped in the hills, on a bed of heather overlooking
Tarbert, pondering my options for the following day. There
were three choices: take the early-afternoon ferry to Skye
and attempt to reach Sligachan in time for the start of the
race up and down Glamaig; take the evening ferry to Skye
and consume my remaining hours on the Long Island by
running the Harris half-marathon; or, the sensible option,
spare myself all running-related physical exertion and take
whatever ferry I fancied.

I would sleep on the matter.

Sleep changed nothing; I was never going to plump for the
latter option. Nor were there any pros to racing on Skye. I
lacked the spirit for mountain running – and Glamaig was a
mountain that required indomitable spirit. I chose the half-
marathon.

I registered, pinned a number to my vest and stood in the
sunshine with 100 others, waiting for buses to transport us
to the start line. We were to be driven to a point 13 miles
away; from there, we would run back to Tarbert. The bus

stopped half-a-mile short of the start line at Borve so runners could relieve themselves among the rocks between the road and sea. 'Ladies to the left, gents to the right,' the driver instructed.

The atmosphere at Borve was breezy. An Edinburgh-based running club, the creatively-named Hunters Bog Trotters, were to the fore, with one of their brown-shirted recruits performing a series of press ups moments before the start. They grunted 'HBT' in unison as the running crowd was despatched. I set off steadily, moving as part of a quartet, allowing the three fastest men to disappear into the distance. For five miles, the race was a joy, run beneath a blue sky, overlooking beaches and machair, passing the jewels of Horgabost, Seilebost and Luskentyre. There is surely no finer half-marathon in Britain, I mused. Repeatedly, I looked west, until Taransay blocked the view; I knew St Kilda was there, hiding beneath the horizon.

As the route turned inland at the start of a two-mile uphill climb, the nation's finest half-marathon became a desperate, demoralising struggle. Limb by limb, muscle by muscle, my body wilted. Press up man drifted in front, as did three or four others, one who was certainly on the wrong side of 50, and then the leading woman. I had visions of the entire field flooding past me until I was at the back of the pack, the last man. A broken figure, I would crawl into Tarbert on bloodied hands and knees after nightfall, hours after the organisers had packed up and gone home. The finish seemed an eternity away.

I stumbled on, stubbornly refusing to walk, despite my shuffling stride being little faster. My will was broken. I knew there would be no second wind. I blamed my shoes – trail shoes that should not be worn on the road for more than a mile or two, and certainly not for 13. But it was not the footwear alone. It was deep-down exhaustion. Events had caught up with me: Goatfell, the Paps of Jura, the Highland Cross, the Inaccessible Pinnacle, Heaval, the sleepless nights, the whisky binges, the sporadic dining habits, the waiting for St Kilda.

As I reached the highest point of the race, Scalpay and the Shiant Isles, surrounded by the glittering water of The Minch, came into view – a vision that lifted my spirits. I ran the last four predominately downhill miles to Tarbert as fast as my aching legs would allow, until I could see the finish line in the ferry car park. Mustering a half-baked sprint finish, I collapsed gladly to the ground. A child handed me a finisher's medal. Lying prostrate on the sun-baked concrete, I promised myself – as I had done during the climax of the Isle of Jura race – that I would never run again.

The ferry was almost an hour late when it departed Tarbert. I sat on the deck shivering. The sun was setting over Harris and Lewis, illuminating the sky in dazzling orange, the last sunset I would see on the islands. For some time a lone gannet was following the ferry to Skye, only to change its mind and swiftly turn back to the Long Island. I wanted to fly with it.

Rain was falling heavily in Uig. Another runner drove me as far as Sligachan, where, mercifully, the rain was marginally less torrential. The sounds of a ceilidh emanated from the Sligachan Hotel. Shouldering my rucksack, I made for a campsite on the opposite side of the road to the hotel, pitching my tent in the beam of the car headlights of another late arrival. I was soon inside my sleeping bag, oblivious to the world outside.

I was wakened by the sound of rain. It was still dark. The gentle pitter-patter of precipitation on a tent roof is not an unattractive noise but a pleasant reverberation that has often lulled me to sleep.

There would be no more sleep tonight. Something was terribly wrong. It was my feet. They were wet, soaking wet, which meant my sleeping bag was wet, which meant the implausible – there was water in my tent. Pulling my hands free of the still-warm reaches of my bag, I rested my palms flat on the floor and slid them tentatively towards my feet. As I passed my knees, both sets of fingers entered water. I continued, with my hands becoming submerged.

I could not see it, but I could feel it: the flood.

I sat up, then motionless, fathomed what to do. It seemed to take an age to decide what was beyond question. I could not stay here; I had to abandon ship. On exit, the problem was immediately apparent: the ground outside was saturated. Pools of water had formed across the site. My tent was positioned in the middle of one. I rolled up the sleeping bag, the sodden goosedown already beginning to reek, and bundled it into the site's laundry room. Going back to my sinking ship, I seized the rest of my dripping belongings and took them to my new home. I returned for a final time to rescue my tent – now empty, apart from the water – from the quagmire. I could not bear to leave the tent where it was. Campers would have passed in the morning, remarking with incredulity that I should site a tent 'there.' But 'there' had seemed perfectly feasible only hours earlier. How was I to know I was pitching my tent on land that would very quickly disappear beneath an ankle-deep covering of water?

Scotland's weather had given me one last hammering, one last kick in the groin.

I waited for dawn: a ghastly, ghostly one when it came. The rain refused to let up. A pall of swirling mist shrink-wrapped Glamaig. Semi-darkness lingered, as if there would be no day today. There was little to do. I put the tumble dryer on to heat the room. I had given up any hope of sleeping. I sat on a wooden surface, staring morosely at a wall, unthinking.

This was no way to end a Hebridean adventure.

More than two hours had slipped past when footsteps outside stirred me from my trance, and a man – the first person I had seen since arriving at Sligachan – strode past the open doorway of the laundry.

I heard more steps soon after, presumably the same person returning to his tent. I directed my gaze to the ground, not wanting to attract attention to myself. After all, I was meant to be sleeping in a tent not squatting in a laundry room.

'Jonny?' I heard a voice question softly.

I glanced up, stunned. 'Dougie?'

A mountain running friend from my time in Inverness, Dougie had come to Sligachan to take part in the Glamaig race. We spoke about islands and mountains, and why I was spending the night in the laundry room of the Sligachan campsite, before Dougie returned to his tent. I resumed my trance, only to be disturbed again soon after by a revisiting Dougie, this time with his wife, Jackie, and a bar of chocolate. The rain had jaded them; their tent had sprung a leak, although its position on higher ground meant they had escaped the flood.

'Home?' Dougie asked. Jackie nodded. Home was Inverness.

'Lift?' he asked me. I nodded gratefully.

Together, in the gloom, we rapidly dismantled their tent. Rain fell like I had never seen it fall before: bucketing, hammering and pouring; a soaked-to-the-skin-in-seconds rain. We drove away from Sligachan with steamed-up windows, shocked at the might of nature. Skye was a cheerless, watery world. Streams of white froth surged off the hills. Raasay and Scalpay were invisible, soaked in mist. We passed signs for Kyleakin, crossed the Skye bridge and drove through Kyle of Lochalsh. The islands of the west were behind me. I was back on the mainland.

The rain continued to fall.

20

London

The World is a book, and those who do not travel read only
a page.

St Augustine

℮

I was standing in front of a howling class of 12 and 13 year-
old boys at a south London secondary school. There were
twenty-three of them. It was late-November, three months
into my apprenticeship as an English teacher. It was the first
lesson after lunch; the students were distracted and fidgety.
My mission – and it truly was a mission – was to introduce
these boys to the themes of Shakespeare's *The Tempest*. In
February, as part of an evening devoted to The Bard, they
would be performing a watered down version before an
audience of their parents and peers.

How do you inspire a class of pre-pubescent boys? How
do you even get them to listen? Planning for the lesson, I had
pondered the central themes of *The Tempest*, speculating on
what might motivate them. I had thought of the obvious –
magic, monsters and slavery – and then it came to me:
islands. *The Tempest* is, after all, set on an isolated, remote
island, possibly located in the Caribbean or the Mediterra-
nean.

I would tell them an island-related story, I decided, the
story of three men and eight boys who were stranded on
Stac an Armin for nine months.

232

As a beginning teacher, I had soon realised that children, generally-speaking, would not do what I would like them to do. They prefer to do the exact opposite. The first five minutes of my lessons tended to follow a similar rigmarole: 'Quiet . . . sit down, quickly . . . bags on the floor . . . no, you can't go to the toilet . . . leave the wasp alone . . . where is your book? . . . you look fine to me . . . leave the curtains alone . . . take your hat off . . . I know it's cold . . . no, I didn't see X Factor . . . no, I don't have a spare pen . . . no, we're not going to do anything fun . . . no, we're not watching a video . . . leave the wasp alone . . . why are you late? . . . sit down, quickly . . . just leave the wasp alone . . .'

A period of cajoling and bribery typically followed, and eventually threats, before at last the boys – most of them – fell silent.

'I am going to tell you a story about an island, a Scottish island.'

'Skye, it's Skye isn't it, sir?' one guessed, his eager, out-stretched arm flailing in the air.

'Why would it be Skye?' I snapped, glaring at the questioner. 'No, it's not Skye.'

'Scotland, bonnie Scotland. Och aye the noo,' another shouted in a mock Glaswegian accent, much to the amusement of his classmates.

'Sir, sir, do they have haggis there?' a different boy cried. They had been obsessed with haggis ever since I had taught a lesson on Robert Burns' *Address to a Haggis*.

'Right, quiet,' I bawled. 'I'm going to tell you a story, a story about an island, an island that I have visited.'

'About Skye?'

'No, not Skye,' I groaned, growing increasingly exasperated, contemplating the abandonment of my tale and making them write in silence instead. One last try. I pressed on: 'This is a story about St Kilda, the most remote island of all the British Isles.'

Before they had time to utter 'St *where?*' or ask if people there ate haggis or attempt further Scottish impressions, I projected an outline of Britain onto the board, using electronic arrows to distinguish London and St Kilda. They hushed, either bored into submission or fathoming the distance between the city and the archipelago.

'But that's, like, just sea, sir,' one boy mumbled.

With the pupils attentive at last, I seized the initiative, launching into my account. The men and boys – 'boys your age', I kept stressing (I had no idea if it was true) – were deposited on an island called Stac an Armin where they would catch and kill cliff-dwelling seabirds. Their fellow St Kildans had been expected to return to the sea rock several days later to collect them, but no boat arrived. I told the class how the 11 survived: slaughtering seabirds, pilfering eggs from nests, catching fish with a pole with a nail in it, drinking rainwater. I told them about the bothy they lived in, the storms that would have lashed their abode, how they skinned birds to make clothes. I told them how the group were eventually rescued nine months later, only to return home to find their families dead; almost all the islanders had succumbed to smallpox.

I came to the end of the story. A true story, non-fiction, I reminded the class, now pin-drop silent. I removed the map of Britain and replaced it with a photograph of Stac an Armin. They gasped, awed by the size of the stack, astonished by the notion that it had once been habitable. A barrage of questions came: who, what, when, why.

The boys were entranced, spellbound. So was I. As I spoke, Stac an Armin became lodged in my mind, this inhospitable needle of rock rising from the ocean, a monstrous representation of human courage. I could taste the salty air. I could feel the swaying motion of being at sea. I could hear the cry of countless birds. The hairs rose on my arms. I trembled inwardly, captivated again by St Kilda. I imagined Stac an Armin on this November afternoon. The light would be fading into gloom; the waves would be continuing their ceaseless, crashing onslaught; mist would be wrapped around the rock. It was a terrible vision, a vision of that other world. Yet I was there again, my senses shaking, back where the isles meet the edge of the sea.

Bibliography

Books and papers

ASKWITH, R. Feet in the Clouds, 2004

BEARHOP, D. Munro's Tables, 1997

BLACK, R. (ed) To the Hebrides: Samuel Johnson's Journey to the Western Islands of Scotland and James Boswell's Journal of a Tour to the Hebrides, 2007

BOURNEMOUTH UNIVERSITY, The Economic Impact of Wildlife Tourism in Scotland, 2010

BUSHBY, K. Giant Steps, 2006

CAMPBELL, R. The Arran Murder of 1889, 2001

DRESSLER, C. Eigg, The Story of an Island, 2007

FULLER, E. The Great Auk: The Extinction of the Original Penguin, 2003

GRIMBLE, I. Scottish Islands, 1988

HASWELL-SMITH, H. The Scottish Islands, 1996

ISLANDS BOOK TRUST, THE. The Decline and Fall of St Kilda, 2005

JANSON, K. Holy Isle, 2007

KRAKAUER, J. Into the Wild, 1998

MACDONALD, A and P. The Hebrides, an aerial view of a cultural landscape, 2010

MACFARLANE, R. The Wild Places, 2008

MACKENZIE, C. Whisky Galore, 1977

MACLEAN, C. Island on the Edge of the World, 2006

MᴄNᴇɪsʜ, C. The Munros, 2003

Mᴀʀᴛɪɴ, M. A Late Voyage to St Kilda, on www.undis-coveredscotland.co.uk, 2010

Mᴜʀʀᴀʏ, W.H. The Companion Guide to the West Highlands of Scotland, 1969

Pᴇʀʀᴏᴛᴛ, D. The Western Islands Handbook, 1998

Sᴄᴏᴛᴛɪsʜ Mᴏᴜɴᴛᴀɪɴᴇᴇʀɪɴɢ Cʟᴜʙ. The Islands of Scotland, 1934

Sᴄᴏᴛᴛɪsʜ Mᴏᴜɴᴛᴀɪɴᴇᴇʀɪɴɢ Cʟᴜʙ. The Island of Skye, 1954

Sᴄᴏᴛᴛɪsʜ Mᴏᴜɴᴛᴀɪɴᴇᴇʀɪɴɢ Cʟᴜʙ. Skye Scrambles, 2000

Sʜᴀᴄᴋʟᴇᴛᴏɴ, E. South, 2007

Sᴛᴇᴇʟ, T. The Life and Death of St Kilda, 1994

Sᴛʀɪᴅᴇ, P. The 1727 St Kilda epidemic: smallpox or chickenpox? 2009

Tʜᴏᴍᴘsᴏɴ, F. Uists and Barra, 1999

Wᴀᴅᴇ Mᴀʀᴛɪɴs, S. Eigg, An Island Landscape, 1987

Media

BBC
Daily Record
Glasgow Herald
Guardian
Independent
London Evening Standard
Oban Times
Press and Journal
Scotsman
Stornoway Gazette
Sun
Times